A FILE ON DEATH

By the same author

SOME BEASTS NO MORE
DEATH AND MR. PRETTYMAN
DEATH AMONG THE STARS
DEATH CRACKS A BOTTLE
MURDER PLUPERFECT

A FILE ON DEATH

A NOVEL

by

KENNETH GILES

WALKER AND COMPANY
New York

Copyright © 1973 by Kenneth Giles

All rights reserved. No part of this book may be reproduced or transmitted in any form or by any means, electronic or mechanical, including photocopying, recording, or by any information storage and retrieval system, without permission in writing from the Publisher.

All the characters and events portrayed in this story are fictitious.

First published in the United States of America in 1973 by the Walker Publishing Company, Inc.

ISBN: 0-8027-5278-0

Library of Congress Catalog Card Number: 72-95799

Printed in the United States of America.

Chapter One

OBESITY HAD BECOME a sore problem to Superintendent Hawker. Retirement and its medical check loomed near: not bearing to think of non-activity and his bleak, echoing house at Wimbledon, filled with memories and the odour of his late wife's addiction to cabbage rolls, the Superintendent pinned his hopes to some sort of grey eminence around Whitehall with his declining years filled with respect and genteel spying for senior ministers. In pursuit of this he had purchased a pair of rubber slimming bloomers which were inflated by a kind of bicycle pump. They made him roll slightly on his chair and emitted strange noises when he stirred violently, but he had great hopes of them. All in all it made worse a temper violent at the best of times and his razor eyes squinted malevolently at Chief Inspector Harry James who was perched in the chair opposite.

"A little bit of delicacy is called for," he snarled, "and God knows whether you've got it, but try. Some documents were purloined from the F.O."

"Top Secret?"

"Old top secrets, which are worse, similar to the Casement Diaries, who arranged to kill Kitchener, the sexual indiscretions of generations of British ministers on trips to Paris—they've got rooms filled with the stuff, guarded by superannuated N.C.O.s with rheumatism and a desire for strong drink. These documents are political. I have copies here. You can't read them, though my long service and honourable scars, plus the fact that this office was bugged three weeks ago by Stealthy Men posing as people from the sanitary department, has entitled me to do so." Hawker leered menacingly but warningly at the bookcase in the corner. "Here is a very brief, succinct as the F.O. label it, synopsis."

It was four hundred words. The Chief Inspector read and blenched.

"Jesus," he said, "we couldn't have ... all those natives ..." and stopped as Hawker's eyes impaled him.

"In one minute and ten seconds, and he is that punctual," said the Superintendent, ogling his Omega, "a Mr. Quarles will be here. He is a gentleman who works in Whitehall. I have known him for twelve years and if you provide results he has a benign nature. If you do not ..." Hawker moved and the room was filled with a trumpeting note. "Damn these bloody things, why can't they fit a silencer? And I should be pumped up again in a quarter of an hour."

There was a tap at the door. James had noticed that the usual civilian major-domo was absent. Hawker creaked up and did his obsequious butler bit, possibly to underline the fact that Mr. Quarles was very important indeed. Physically the visitor was of medium height with a perfectly round face, otherwise anything that could be guessed of him was in elongated ovals, from his pouter-pigeon chest to his pot belly. His smile was vague but permanently fixed. He strutted rather than walked and he clutched Harry's proffered hand in a surprisingly rough grip.

"I know of you, Chief Inspector, your works preceding our acquaintance."

Quarles took a seat and looked about him. "I suppose, Super, that Mr. James has been informed of the circumstances."

Hawker said, without enthusiasm, "He looked through the précis a couple of minutes ago."

"And was shocked, of course." Quarles' amber eyes caressed the Chief Inspector with joviality."

"Well..."

"You've come to a kind of ridge," said Quarles in his sweet baritone. "Many men never achieve it, Mr. James. I'll give you two horrid clichés: one, things have to be done for Reasons of State; two, the underlings, like us, do not reason why. If you will not swallow this professional bolus, just tell me now. Sit back and think."

The Chief Inspector's initial flush of indignation had suddenly become assuaged by thoughts of a Superintendentship, upon retirement some juicy little preferment, say an Inspector of Prisons, fiscal security for his family, and, what the hell, he did not run the country anyway.

"Well, it was rather a shock."

"Hindsight always is," agreed Quarles. "You are well aware that decisions are pragmatically taken on the basis of *known facts* and facts unfortunately alter. Some of the most valuable men in this country were, before your time, Men of Munich, vulgarly so called. Now that we have little Munichs every week their experience puts us ahead, say, of the Americans or any other friendly competitor. The paper you saw is not pleasant, no indeed, but at the time," his plump hands stroked his coat front, "it seemed best for the State."

"I just catch criminals, civilian criminals."

"Very good. I shall dine out on that. Well put indeed! Nevertheless the work has to be done. As a person of high I.Q. you can envisage what would be the effect of the documents' publication in the vulgar press, or, worse still, a respectable journal. Both parties are implicated: it would mean a chaotic election."

"Surely the Official Secrets Act would cover it? I mean they put Compton Mackenzie on trial."

"The press millionaires, my dear sir, can become inflamed by missionary zeal, and they don't go on trial anywhere, merely some unfortunate journalists and printers. Crusades in the 'public interest' are best conducted from Bermuda where there is little personal taxation and difficult extradition. These papers would be printed, and even if not here their impact abroad would be equally explosive. If they were published in the States, journals here could quote with impunity, proceedings being virtually impossible."

"There are the..." Harry stopped, realising Mr. Quarles' possible role in life.

"The Stealthy Men. Oh, yes," Quarles soothed his belly with one forearm and Harry diagnosed butterflies. "My dear sir, everybody has had a go at it except Scotland Yard. I'd better explain myself. You may ask why such documents are ever kept, and I can only plead that Man has an inborn passion to commit himself to paper. A junior minister had expressed a desire to see the papers and I have no idea why except that history might be on its way to repeat itself in a similar region. They were taken to his office by one ex-Quartermaster Sergeant Wortleberry, aged sixty-three, much decorated, lives with his eldest son and is devoted to football pools, steak-and-kidney and draught bass, roughly in that order. He remained in the minister's room for an hour, relocked the papers in the special case handcuffed to his left wrist, and went back to the archives. It was one thirty and I think the Sergeant was thinking of his meal which he takes in a snug little pub off Charing Cross where he has a weekly arrangement. He usually gets there at ten minutes past one, being a man of habit.

"You must understand that while we do not go to the extent of the U.S. security check, we do take basic precautions. If you were an alcoholic pederast, heavily in debt, and given to hanging around the gates of the Russian Embassy, you would be translated to the office which supervises tinned food supplies to our embassies and establishments abroad. Now at the reception desk in the archives there was some confusion. It is a dark office and a fuse had blown. A report indicates that something might have been deliberately shorted. In any case various staff were going out to lunch, the wash room was at full spate, and the customary calm did not prevail. It was something that might have been foreseen, but you cannot in practice plug all the holes. Sergeant Wortleberry gave the papers to the presiding clerk, who signed the necessary docket. The Sergeant departed for his steak-and-kidney and the clerk placed the papers in a chute which leads into a kind of locked box emptied every hour by two men who do the requisite filing. Or so he says, because the documents have not been sighted since. What we have are microfilms.

"The clerk is a certain Gough Trengold, a man of forty-seven. He lives at Clapham with his wife and two boys aged twenty and eighteen. Not liked by his family, a reciprocal feeling, he is a rather heavy drinker and a morose person who feels that his rather expensive education has not been rewarded and that, inebriated by lust, he married beneath him twenty-two years ago."

"You must have dug pretty deep," commented Harry James.

"We did exactly that, to the extent of getting copies of his old school reports. God knows what went wrong with him, nothing ideological. He had a kind of block about passing exams plus an inbuilt capacity for annoying his mentors. He likes the company of his social inferiors and has a subtle, biting wit. A character! That was what his workmates summed him up as. All the scatological remarks in the department could be traced back to Trengold. And he hates everybody. As you say we had to dig to get that point out. There is no political association: merely personal egotism."

"Why these papers?"

"Did you read contemporary history?"

"Well, no, Mr. Quarles."

"There are scores of documents that we, with hindsight, cannot allow the public to read, and *for their own good*. Virtuous indignation is all very well, but no cure for radio-active drinking water. We think that Trengold knew that on any day something embarrassing would go through the works and was lucky in that this was particularly juicy."

"I suppose the usual pressure has been brought to bear?"

"He's been psyched to the best of our skill. He can hardly go into a pub without being palled up by an equally bitter-tongued man. A female agent who can seduce Greek statuary if ordered slipped on a banana skin in front of him, but no go. He dislikes the human race too much. But you can see the file on Trengold. He has been called up officially, but quite calmly denies all knowledge. He supposes a file was returned and that he signed for it, in which case he would have placed it in the chute. Stalemate! He is solvent, with about four hundred pounds represented by bank deposits and insurance. He lives in a rented flat and spends a little less than his income. No car, two suits a year, non-smoker, allows more than he should afford on drink, but no other discernible vices. Attitudes are cynical, and bitterly negative. You will realise that many public servants are underpaid, but are sustained by some vague thought of civic duty. A lot of them become, let's say rather snappy in con-versation, perhaps a trifle inclined to bear down on the public where possible . . . Trengold is the odd card in that pack."

"Is the name foreign?"

"Not that we can tell, as far back as 1800. He came from Lancashire and was minor public school and university, with a pass B.A. His father manufactured fancy buttons, but retired with very little. There is a younger brother who farms on a small scale and an elder sister married to an assistant town clerk. No leads at all there. Gough Trengold has never travelled outside the country, by the way, and we thought at first that it might be significant but it proved not to be the case. He did badly in exams and ended up where he is."

"Then he *is* Gough Trengold!"

"No question at all of his identity: we could not check the cradle or the grave, but in between has been double-checked at the expense of around twenty thousand pounds. What we think he did was to place the eight hundred pages in a previously prepared and stamped envelope and stick it in a post box on his way to lunch. Thereon hangs our only clue. It would have cost him twenty pence to post but he had put on one hundred pence. Obviously he could not have judged in advance the weight of the evidence, shall we say, and getting it weighed represented a small risk which he preferred to avoid. It happened that the manual sorter in the post office noticed it and made a joke to his mate about people chucking away money. He has a professionally visual memory and the envelope was addressed to Sir Hugh Palabras, at Waddington Parva, near Granchester. At any rate we think it was the packet."

Harry chewed his upper lip. Palabras, holder of a James One baronetcy, was a magnificent failure, a recluse who sent brilliant but vicious letters to any newspaper or magazine who would publish them, mainly half jokingly because over the years Sir Hugh had become a public butt, founder of foundered political parties and societies, possessor of some bleary-eyed theory concerning an élite based on intelligence tests who alone would be allowed to breed. The Chief Inspector remembered that Sir Hugh, a millionaire bachelor, was alleged to allow himself this concession pretty freely.

"He denies it?"

"We never asked. Since the papers went off he has lived quietly at Waddington Parva: we managed to get an under parlourmaid in, he lives very grandly indeed. That is part of the trouble: international celebrities of the crankier kind weekend prolifically at Sir Hugh's. Magnificent food and wine, billiards, tennis, riding, shooting, fishing, fornication in a civilised way and if you name it Sir Hugh can get it. He is in fact eighteenth century, as he proclaims. One conclusion is that Sir Hugh would delight to send this country into chaos. The other is that he is in part stuck with it, because in the past he has issued so many false or ill-judged manifestos that editors, broadcasters and even the public take anything he says with a pretty large grain of salt. After all he did accuse Sir Winston of a great many things, some of which one is afraid were German 'plants'. That was in his vigorous days, he is in his late sixties now and rather more hesitant to dash into the fray."

"How long has it been?"

"Seven months. I must say that the papers ring of authenticity and Sir Hugh in spite of his eccentricity is a veritable mine of facts. But what makes us so uneasy is a tip-off." Quarles put his fingertips together. "The world seems filled with people eager to make a swift penny out of monetary speculation—one cannot blame them I suppose—and we have quite a few contacts among the professionals. Our best sources are in the Middle East where the oil money floats around and our information is that some kind of diplomatic bomb is due to go off in two months' time, preceded by massive selling of the pound sterling. The man who brought it to us, a Syrian, was killed three days later in a hit-and-run accident in Tripoli." He shrugged. "He was a double agent but as far as it went his stuff was first class. There have been other rumours scuttling around, but, there again, we hear so many. Somebody makes up a pretty story in a Lisbon bar, a professional pryer hears part of it over the general noise, knocks it into shape and flogs it to one of our Embassy men for twenty pounds."

"Couldn't you . . ."

"Now, laddie, we don't talk of such things. Sir Hugh has good locks on his doors. He does not drive a car, otherwise he could be pulled in for drunken driving and his house inspected. He has a brilliant brain of sorts and has taken every precaution. Remember that! And he is one of these men," Mr. Quarles beamed lovingly, "who are never more dangerous than when pleasant."

The pot and the kettle, thought Harry.

"I take it," said the Chief Inspector, "that the usual Stealthy channels, the flapping-ears-in-bars bit, the suborning of servants, the tapping of wires and steaming open of envelopes, the hiring of reliable whores, the procuration of amenable guardsmen, the administration of truth drugs in glasses of dry sherry, the recruitment of monstrous regiments of professional blackmailers and bludgers, have been to no avail." He felt his neck getting red.

"You'll do, laddie, when it's rubbed off a bit," responded Mr. Quarles admiringly. "No, we haven't got a sausage and the best whore in London, if you can call her that because she does it only for patriotic reasons, staff officers on leave and selected M.P.s, has been sleeping with him for two months. The cunning old swine always locks the door to his private suite and tapes the key under his left armpit."

"Then, why me?"

"There is a pub called the Marquis of Tenterton at Waddington Parva, rather a good one, artily rebuilt for the tourist trade. A man named Justin Title died there two days ago, in his room with a nice clean overdose of brandy and barbiturates, the usual suicide prescription. The Chief Constable does not like it, although the bedroom was locked from inside. There was no suicide note and Title was a eupeptic Irishman who'd dined at seven, taken two slow beers in the lounge and gone to bed around ten thirty. He had arrived on the Monday, and died Saturday night."

"And the point?" asked Harry wearily.

Hawker squirmed with unnerving results. His bloomers were palpably deflating and even he looked embarrassed as he said, "He spent two hours with Sir Hugh on the Wednesday. Oh, the locals saw the blessed baronet who said that Justin Title was peddling an interesting new system of burglar alarms. The company exists and Title worked for them on commission: they had not sent him to Waddington Parva and did not pay expenses if a sale was not completed."

The old Super extracted a file from his drawer. "You can have this later. Briefly Title was an Irishman from Cork, whose loquacity had earned him the title of 'the talking machine'. Adrift from his kin—his father keeps a grocery and beer shop and his brothers are civil servants. We knew of him, but there was no criminal record. He was potentially of interest because he would take anything on, but like a barrister somebody had to supply a brief and he was not legally responsible for what he said—any goddamned lie as long as he had written instructions, which he took care to have. Three years in Australia selling mining stock, a stint in South Africa, maybe other places we don't know about. He had 'inadvertently' burnt his Irish passport four times and applied for new ones, which is what they all do, but Interpol picked up a bit from his international driver's licence and insurance applications. He was a well-known night-club figure in Amsterdam. Thirty-eight years of age, slightly built, with a strong attractive brogue and the stage-Irishman act. No hint of violence, and he seems to have been well educated somewhere along the line. Title could have made a good con man, but he kept this side of it. He lived in a good-class private hotel: manner of life probably fifty pounds a week after tax, which he obviously fiddled. I don't relish the case much. The barmaids describe Title as a retiring sort of fellow who did not speak much. That was dead out of character. He must have been up to something very fishy.

"He spent the evenings either out of the hotel or in his room—there were six paperbacks, biographies, on the writing desk. The bottle was a quarter empty. Title does not appear to have had a drink problem, by the way, although he used to like a brandy before going to bed. Nobody at the Marquis of Tenterton recalls selling him it, so he probably brought it in with him in his suitcase. The drugs were dissolved in the bottle."

"Drugs... plural," exclaimed Harry.

"There were about four, perhaps five, types of sleeping pill dissolved, representing around one hundred tablets, all of which would be subject to doctor's prescription. It's quite common," Hawker turned to Quarles, "for people contemplating suicide to squirrel away a few tablets at a time. Often they have nervous disorders for which pills are prescribed. They think, the path boys that is, that he ingurgitated two ounces of brandy around ten on Friday night. He would have felt woozy soon after. Evidently he lay fully dressed on the bed. A chambermaid called the landlord at ten next day. The key was on the inside and finally they used a crowbar on the door. Title was blue in the face and barely breathing. He died fifteen minutes after they got him to hospital. One thing has been established—he carried his private business under his hat. He worked on a commission basis for several reputable firms who get the potential client as the result of small ads, the burglar-alarm company for one. Alternatively there was cut-price car insurance for firms with medium-sized fleets, a ventilation system for churches and properties for sale on the Costa Brava. It was, one supposes, a magnificent cover for more dubious exercises, and one way or another it could get him in practically anywhere. At that he probably made a quarter of his income at it, though one company says he worked in a casual, desultory way."

"And you think he had business with Sir Hugh Palabras, with the burglar-alarm scheme as a cover?"

"Not necessarily," said Quarles, interposing a little testily. "As you'll see from the file, Title had curious contacts. I should say that if you wanted a report on a house, how it would stand up to burglary for instance, he would have got it for a fee, being careful not to know the criminal intention. It's even money that he got fed up with himself and took the pill way to oblivion. However, in taking the opportunity to enquire into his death, you could get an innocent entrée into Sir Hugh's ancestral pile, named Firbank. It's a chance, and we leap at small straws now."

"Even if we got the original back, Sir Hugh would have made photostats, any fool can acquire the expertise nowadays."

"M'dear fellow," said Quarles, grease on his tongue, "without the original about we'd deny it as a Russian forgery. But anyhow, suppose you have a free hand for a week, money no object but if you have to bribe, five hundred is the top unless cleared through the Superintendent here. Take whatever transport you like."

"A nondescript Volks is what I like," said Harry. "I suppose I can take my Sergeant."

Hawker rolled his eyes. "If beer is the criterion, the case will take three days."

"He knows the district, the family coming from Dorset."

"It might be an idea," said the omniscient Quarles. "Palabras keeps a superior servants' hall, not the old brown-painted basement, but a flash job with T.V. and a large fridge and his butler and staff like their drop within reason; the younger females are no better than they ought to be, but all are intensely loyal to the master who, having no heirs, lives better than a lord and has a generous staff retirement plan. Your Sergeant might wheedle his way where Chief Inspectors fear to tread. We frankly got nowhere. As I said we've got an under parlourmaid on the payroll, a Miss Stinting, who has learned nothing except some traumatic propositions from a visiting German Christian Socialist."

"Stay at the pub," counselled Hawker, "quite openly, of course. See Palabras tomorrow."

"I see you're wearing one of those garments," ingratiated Quarles as the door closed. "They are all the rage in our shop as the Minister is so keen on athletics. I'll blow you up if you like."

Hawker totally subsided in a vast postern blast. He eyed Quarles unfavourably. "I have a uniformed constable, if necessary, to refill the apparatus . . . I suppose you are staking the Chief Inspector out as a goat."

"Well, there does not seem any other way. Scotland Yard might alarm them."

"You mean the Russians, Arabs, etcetera, who would have an interest in seeing the papers published!"

'Two Dublin boys have disappeared from our surveillance, both very slick experts at removals."

"I've known James these seven years," Hawker was

doubly uncomfortable, "plus his charming wife and beastly kids."

"It's always difficult," said Quarles, "but under the rule he would be stepped up posthumously to Chief Superintendent and the pension paid three months back, a rare solace to the widow."

"I might see you for lunch at the club," said Hawker, who had no intention of so doing.

Chapter Two

Harry James had regretted his choice of the almost invisible Volks because Sergeant Honeybody, meeting a wartime acquaintance, had lunched off a virulent selection of garlic sausage washed down by chianti and insisted on talking—scatological anecdotes—the whole mortal way down, a process which they accomplished by 5 p.m. The Marquis of Tenterton, where most of the Victorian literary bores had stayed according to a plaque, had been rebuilt in 1955 and was a splendid bit of Tudor fakery with so many loos that Honeybody conjectured that the architect must have been gone in the bladder. The landlord, a ponderous man called 'Bosky' Lane, regretted that even to oblige the Chief Constable he could only provide two narrow-gutted rooms at the back of the third floor, overlooking the green village duckpond which smelled rather high at noon.

If you wish to recruit young ladies for light but profitable duties on the sunny beaches of Spain, to peddle West Indian investments returning twenty per cent guaranteed by a benevolent population, wheedle the charitable into subscribing funds for the hands of oriental officials or just plain burglarise, it is wise to see the Vicar or Rector first, or, in dire straits in poorer parishes, the Curate. Innocent but talkative, they are a mine of information and the call itself sets a local seal on respectability.

So, refusing Honeybody's pleas to inspect the three bars, Harry set off with his assistant to catch the Vicar before dinner. The Vicarage was cramped between old stabling, possessed a hideous tower, and was the other side of the duck-pond. Hawker's file stated that it was a nice living, possessed of a Norman church falling down in parts and a congregation of seventeen including the organist. The incumbent, a Dr. Tulkingham, was interested in birds. After they had hammered at the large door, itself riven by cracks on its unvarnished surface and bereft of a bell, a small woman with steel-rimmed glasses and a built-in air of alarm answered it and said that the Vicar would probably see them if they would come this way.

Dr. Tulkingham sat in slippered ease among stuffed birds. One, looking particularly dead, he was stuffing with a forcing bag filled with sawdust. He was a plump little man with buck teeth reinforced with gold fillings.

The preliminaries over, Harry addressed him with the false heartiness reserved for vicars. "I think I may have read an ornithological paper of yours, sir."

Dr. Tulkingham gave a kind of sit-down curtsy, but said modestly, "I now confine myself to Whimbrels, Blacktailed Godwits, and Gadwalls, with occasionally a side glance, as it were, at my old friends the Shovellers. As you may see, I'm doing a Shoveller at the moment."

"Whimbrels," said Sergeant Honeybody, in the piteous tone which abstention from alcohol produced.

The Vicar took it as general conversation. "One is tempted by Tufted Ducks, but, alas, specialisation is the tone of the age and one has a limited time for stuffing, sickness in the parish, unemployment and drink being rampant."

"I understand one Justin Title saw you five days ago."

The Vicar's eyes, noted Harry, were hard and shrewd and blue.

"We get strange callers, Chief Inspector, some very strange ones. It is one of the Crosses of the profession. Deceased, poor fellow, was very specious and one wondered what he was after. Ventilation, he said, but with the small congregations the Age produces plus National Health, there is not much problem. A small quantity of incense, not enough to offend our low members, suffices. He talked a great deal and one took the precaution, after he had gone, of ringing up the firm he represented. All seemed to be in order, though they were cautious." His capable hands were now affixing the Shoveller to a piece of board. "The eyes are very difficult," he said, "the best being made in Japan but hard to get. Mrs. Tulkingham soaks currants in one of the new fast-setting glues, which is a considerable saving."

Harry could not resist the question, "What do you do with the birds, padre?"

"Small ads in the *Observer*, 'a bird for three guineas boxed' producing remarkable results. The Whimbrels are most popular."

"Boxed," said Honeybody, a dismal chorus.

"There seem to be some peculiarities about Mr. Title's demise," said Harry.

"Death is always peculiar," said Dr. Tulkingham amiably, twisting the Shoveller's beak into a more entertaining position. "Naturally one sees a great deal of it, people neglecting us for years except for matrimony and childbirth and then requiring Solace in the last dread moments." He produced a tiny spray-gun from a drawer and started to touch up the Shoveller.

"Ladies' hair lacquer," said the Vicar in response to Sergeant Honeybody's goggle, "though we use car spray for the greens, of course."

The Chief Inspector, accustomed as he was to strange odours in the way of duty, became conscious that the room did niff of dead poultry and lacquer in an unpleasant combination. "Did the late Title have anything to ask particularly?"

"The Squire, Sir Hugh Palabras, was his main consideration. He tried to disguise the fact, but after listening to every kind of prevarication during my ministry, one gets used to spotting such things as a matter of course. I had very promptly assured him as he came in that we have no spare funds in the parish"—to Harry's experienced eye the Vicar looked a bit dodgy—"and he smoothly got on the subject of wealthy benefactors and mentioned Sir Hugh who attends the Cathedral when he thinks of it but certainly not my church. Every year Sir Hugh contributes one hundred guineas to my nave, which is in a parlous condition, and once a year the ladies have a sale of work under the trees around the duckpond, but unless we get a grant one fears for the nave."

Honeybody was looking stunned. Harry asked, "What kind of a man is Sir Hugh?"

"The Palabras fortunes came from Cornish tin; an ill-favoured bride from the north brought with her a square mile of rock which in the last century proved to be coal; another unfortunate match, so it was thought at the time, brought what is now twenty acres of skyscraper west of Piccadilly Circus. Hugh admires the eighteenth century and has opinions about Blood and the Duties of the Lower Orders which are not in keeping with the views of the Age except that he is lax on the subject of fornication which endears him to the youth of the village."

"Unmarried, I think," Harry essayed a man-to-man leer, "so I suppose there is a mistress..."

"Lemans," said the Vicar, putting the last touch to the Shoveller. "He has a succession of lemans; he goes to the Cathedral, let the Bishop deal with him! If you will excuse me, I have a man calling with an allegedly well-preserved Widgeon, a rarity. The American Embassy enquired of me about one, the Eagle having become unpopular these days, and somebody was telling me that there is a Reeve in the garden of the Marquis of Tenterton. Should you see it, pray inform me, for there is a small but steady demand for Reeves."

"I can't work it out, Harry," said Honeybody as they walked round the duckpond.

"He must make a hundred quid a week on the sly selling stuffed birds. The Scouts would catch them for him at two bob a time and then it's a squirt of sawdust and lacquer."

"It's not that, but it's Sir Hugh with lemons. I mean I know these stories about the Arabs, but a lemon . . . with all those pips and with . . ."

"L-e-m-a-n, a godly way to spell girl-friend."

"Oh, normal," said Honeybody, disappointment in his voice.

"If anything is normal." The Chief Inspector scowled at a passing duck as they neared the side entrance of the pub, outpaced by the Sergeant who was nearing the bottom of a pint of Red Barrel by the time his superior had washed his hands.

As Harry joined him he was on terms of calling the generously built barmaid, 'my old dear', and enquiring whether she had a twin sister in Wigan. Less adept at such matters, Harry settled for a gin-and-tonic, ordered steak for dinner, and asked the lady if she had known the late Justin Title.

"A quiet gentleman," she opined, "with hisself to hisself, like, but we get to know them behind the pumps and he wasn't rilly."

"The quiet ones are always the worst, like a certain person." Honeybody, at his most revolting self, ogled the barmaid with his small twinkling eyes and she bridled back.

"Like another certain person," she said, "I would not have

trusted him. There was a man like him who sold my dad a set of encyclopaedias published in eighteen ninety-two. If I'd seen him cottoning on to a customer I might have asked the guv to Drop a Word, though it's difficult to do, people being so silly, but as I said he never had more than half a pint, which is less than other certain persons." Honeybody had been flourishing an empty glass.

"Perhaps he had something on his mind," insinuated Harry.

She replenished the Sergeant's glass. "He was quite relaxed, but just not talking. He might have been the kind of guy who only talks when he wants something."

"He wasn't," said Harry. "He was a compulsive talker."

"That's bad, dear," she said, "when they bottle it up. So he ups and poisons hisself, not but that they take so many pills these days that they can do it by mistake."

The Chief Inspector was fascinated momentarily by her disassociation from life the other side of her bit of bar space.

"He always was served by you?"

She laughed. "There are only two of us on here of an evening, and I don't work in the day. He usually stood just where you are for perhaps twenty minutes."

"I hope you are not going to gossip to my staff all the mortal night and day!" It was the licensee, Bosky Lane.

He would bully when he could, thought Harry, but Honeybody got in first. "It's news to me that paying visitors aren't allowed to talk to staff, and I expect the licensing justices might be surprised."

"What wags we all be," Lane laughed with professional bonhomie, but he had accomplished his purpose as the barmaid moved off.

"We'll have to call you at the inquest," said Harry.

"What little I know of it is common knowledge," said Lane.

A FILE ON DEATH

"He only stayed here the once?"

"He was here six months ago for three nights. It's like this, we do a big passing room trade. People get off the highway and drive the four miles here, all sorts nowadays, but including a lot of travellers going west who want a steak, a drink or two and early to bed. We serve breakfast from six until nine. I thought that Title was a commercial traveller of the better class, judging by his car and the quality of his suit. You get to assess such things automatically. Here! Have one on me before you go in to dinner—when you won't be disappointed because the chef is a dago and good at the sauces: very tasty they are. Miss! Fill again and a small bitter for me.

"Title was in the back of my mind as an earwig, a curse of the profession. I would have sworn that six months ago he had me backed into a corner and was yabbering like two Barbary apes, about what I have no recollection. So when I saw him at the reception desk, I winced, but he had quite changed. He was laconic, that is the word."

"There was a booking?"

"Lord, yes, we could do with another thirty rooms, in fact the Estate is going to put them on. It was a telephone call three days previous. Generally it's last-minute bookings with us and we don't have much trouble fitting people in at three days."

"What the devil was he doing here?" asked Harry.

"The butcher said he was travelling in church fittings, him being a warden. We get a few of them, there being a lot of money in holy statues and the like among the Catholics and high church. Mostly around here they are free church and God knows what my trade would be but for the gentry and the passers-by. The locals don't change a shirt or a fiver over three months."

"Sir Hugh comes here, I suppose. Sir Hugh Palabras," said Harry as Lane looked blank.

"I must be going, gentlemen." The landlord's big face creased into a valedictory smile as he went away through the crowded bar.

"We'd better eat," said Harry, firmly taking Honeybody's pot from his hand, "and I'll stand an Australian hock with the steak, red being likely to inflame your passions in regard to the barmaid."

However the fish soup was so good, and the people at the next table were devouring their steaks with such cannibalistic enthusiasm, that Harry relented and ordered a modest Spanish red. You had to be a Super or have private means before 'they' authorised French. Honeybody's large red face crinkled in the pleasure lines that what he called 'a good table' always produced and he had his serviette well tucked into his blue serge waistcoat.

"They are a funny lot," said the Sergeant when the steaks and béarnaise sauce had been united on their plates and he had taken a contented mouthful. "A vicar that fiddles, a wicked squire that is morally loose, and a landlord I would not trust an inch."

"And rattling good steak, to say nothing of the trimmings." In spite of his words the Chief Inspector was troubled, for Honeybody's nose, though on the reddish side, had an abnormal capacity to smell trouble.

Eating steadily, the Sergeant let his small, shrewd eyes roam the room and he didn't speak until the apple tart was on the table. Then he said, quietly. "There's a woman of a bit under thirty by herself at a table three away from the servery door. I know her and she knows me."

Harry looked in the opposite direction and then allowed his eyes to drift back. The lady was red haired, probably naturally judging by her skin, greenish eyed, a bit overweight and excellently groomed. For a moment her eyes met his. A pro of some sort, registered Harry.

"Name's Dianile Higgins," said Honeybody, "and a smart operator. I did a bit of work on a case two years back when a bloke alleged he was framed in a divorce case. His wife had employed a private detective and adultery had been proved in Amsterdam. He decided to cut his losses but we were asked to poke around a bit. Dianile was the girl who opened the door and used a flashlight camera. The man said he was drugged and lured into the room, which he might have been. Dianile speaks six languages, her father and mother—quite respectable—having moved about a lot for U.N.O. If you want information from across the Channel the agency puts Dianile on the assignment. She has connections, and the Treasury have her on their file of people who illicitly transfer money . . . you know, you hand ten thousand over in London and it can turn up anywhere you like."

"I thought that game was a bit passé," said Harry, "too much risk incurred these days."

"I meant it past tense, about six years ago it was. Diamonds and dope have also been mentioned in connection with the lady. Anyway the judge wasn't satisfied and I went over to see her at her flat in Knightsbridge where she played it dead cool. Some smart lawyer must have briefed her, so the Crown Solicitor's man said when we put it to him, for there was not the smell of a case that we could bring."

"She must be coining it."

"A very nice flat with the new Jag in the garage," said Honeybody.

"A man?"

"We didn't enquire that far. The case was closed the day after my first report."

Harry sighed for generally in crookdom the female is the more difficult to catch.

"I did not tell you exactly what we are after, Honeybody."

"Quite enough, and I guessed the rest. Political stuff. Argh!" The Sergeant produced a toothpick from his waistcoat pocket. "You want to watch or they'll job you on that, Harry. During the Korean business I picked up somebody who turned out to be a Jap waiter and the document was a careful list of what he was buying at the market for the boss. They transferred me to Brixton for three months, not that it wasn't interesting because..." Harry listened as he chewed. Occasionally Honeybody's scabrous anecdotes were soothing.

Miss Higgins finished her meal quickly and Harry noticed that she paid cash before she went out, studiously avoiding his gaze. There was no secrecy now. If you were observed the text-book rule was to try to scare them.

"We'd better see Bosky Lane," said the Chief Inspector and signed the bill in defiance of Honeybody's pleas for welsh rarebit and a trial run of the house port. It took a little time to catch the waiter's bored eye.

Miss Higgins, a small case by her feet, was settling up with the proprietor at the reception desk. "The car's outside," she said, "and I can take the case myself. I paid for dinner."

There was nothing for it but to watch her go. "This lady, the one who has just left, when did she arrive?" Harry asked.

Lane looked at them absently as he pushed closed the drawer of the cash register. "Two days ago. A Miss Higgins, a tourist, I think, visiting our beauty spots."

"Like the duckpond?"

"Now, Inspector, you haven't seen us in our full majesty so to speak, the thatched cottages, General Gould, the Master, on his great bay gelding and his hounds in full cry before him. Granted it rains a lot, but the smell of rain on the upturned sod..." There was a momentary screech outside and the Chief Inspector wondered whether the hounds killed nightly outside the Marquis of Tenterton, possibly egged on by the Vicar as well as bloodthirsty old military gentlemen. Instead a tall woman burst through the door. Some trick of symmetry made her completely round head look abnormally small.

"Miss Sloper," said the landlord, "your table is still reserved, though you are late."

She had a precise, rather guttural voice. "A woman outside has been hit by a car. Doctor, ambulance and police at once!"

Lane took up the handset and Harry preceded the Sergeant through the door. A green car was parked and beyond the driver's door lay Miss Higgins, blood oozing from her nose. Her eyes were closed. Harry bent and took her pulse: it was fairly strong. "Stay there," he told Honeybody and returned to Miss Sloper and the landlord.

"I'm a police officer."

Miss Sloper said, concisely, "I live nearby. I was about to cross the road when I saw a woman carrying a suitcase. She put it down, I thought to open the door. A grey car, travelling in the direction of Granchester, came up fast. I stepped out and waved my hand, but it side-swiped her and drove on. I did not get the number because of the glare in my eyes."

"An accident you think?"

"What else?" Miss Sloper shrugged. "Nothing I can do, because if not I'll get my dinner?"

"We'll have to take a statement in the morning and thank you."

"I told the local police about the grey car," said Lane as Harry reached for the phone. "A very capable lady," he lowered his voice as he watched the head waiter open the door of the dining-room.

"Resident?"

"A delightful eighteenth-century abode on the Palabras Estate, left to her by her old Auntie who was a head of the Girl Guides." Lane said it as though it proved respectability. "Miss Sloper is the church organist, runs the Village Institute, is secretary of the Women's Pleasant Hour, is an honorary district visitor to the Women's Prison over at Granchester. I do not really know what we would do without Miss Sloper." The landlord massaged his great nose as the howl of an ambulance interrupted him. A uniformed police sergeant came through the door.

Harry got out a card. "C.I.D."

"I had the pleasure of meeting Sergeant Honeybody before, sir."

Harry noted that he looked like a drinker and sighed.

"We know the lady, Sergeant, one Miss Higgins. What is the report?"

"Smashed nose, concussion, broken wrist. The quack doesn't think there is much else but bruising, though the concussion could be serious."

"I'll phone London. We have her address. There are parents somewhere."

"Known to you people was she?" said Lane wrinkling his lips as though he had tasted vinegar. "This sort of thing gets a house a bad name. You get the sensation-mongers, but overall the effect is bad. The Estate won't be pleased if there is publicity."

"I'm sure there will be co-operation," soothed the local Sergeant.

"What Estate?" queried the Chief Inspector irritably.

"That of Sir Hugh Palabras, sir. He owns the pub along with the Granchester Brewery and forty other houses."

* * *

In a small side room which smelled of damp washing, Honeybody and the Chief Inspector, a bottle of Scotch on the ironing table, sat on kitchen chairs examining Miss Higgins' overnight bag and other personal effects. It was midnight and the Chief Inspector was looking at the lady's passport. "Bobs about like a yo-yo," he commented. "Got back from a four-day stop-over at Lucerne ten days ago. Before that Paris and Zurich all within a month. An operator, obviously, probably connected with The Outfit if there is a dope side to it. And this letter..."

The handwriting was big, bold and in green ink. It said: "Darl, the place is wide open though the old fool thinks not. There is a very obvious safe behind a Dutch painting in the workroom. It is there I would imagine. Servants except one elderly man sleep out, going around eleven. Sir Hugh sleeps in a separate suite, door of which could be jammed on the outside. Telephone wires visible from the outside. Doors and windows wired, tee-hee, by my old friends, Blackstoke Ltd. Perhaps Charlie & Co. Love, love and longing, Ever J."

"Justin Title in all prob," said Honeybody, refreshing himself, "the pro Irish often using green ink, typewriter ribbons and the like. It would have been a good combine, him and her. Oh, the mysteries of the human heart!"

"Be fair about that Scotch, Honeybody," admonished the Chief Inspector. "Drink fair is all one can expect in this life."

"Blackstokes are burglar alarms," said Honeybody, as Harry poured for himself, "and too scientific to be true or accurate. Wonderful promotions, but any cheap thief can get into a Blackstoke Guarded House, which is their gimmick."

"Who was employing Title?"

"We won't find out from anything he left behind," said the Sergeant. "I know 'em too well, the Irish boys. All the talk is done in a pub, and there the money changes hands.

The woman might be different, they having a passion for book-keeping. But, I'll tell you something: when she was laid out on the tarmac waiting for the ambulance she was feigning."

"You sure?"

"I had eight months on traffic and scooped them up like jelly. She closed her eyes because she didn't want to talk. No neck injuries which shut you up, and I'm ninety per cent sure. I've seen too many injured parties to make much of a mistake."

"We'll see," grunted Harry. "This Charlie & Co. would be Charlie Welch."

"He comes expensive," said Honeybody, trying to pluck up courage to broach the bottle once more.

"As you are meeting that barmaid to the north of the duckpond by the church porch at one you'd better keep off the gravy," said Harry, unpleasantly.

"It doesn't affect me in matters of affection," leered the Sergeant.

"Charlie Welch," mused Harry, giving it up as a bad job. "A standover man from Melbourne, Australia. A gunman as he'd have been known here. He lost his appetite for violence after somebody chased him with an automatic rifle and came here as a fixer. Whatever you want Chas. can get, in this case I would guess a capable burglar and the necessary assistants."

"He tells a good anecdote, does Chas.," said Honeybody, "and likes his drop and a good table. I suppose I could see him. He always gives a dry sherry and smoked salmon nosh on Wednesdays at one o'clock. As much as you can take and a hire-car contract to ensure you get home. All the best thieves are there and the more attractive madams because Chas. throws a lot of work in their way."

"If anybody sees Chas. I shall."

"And you a young married man!" Honeybody looked shocked.

The room which Bosky Lane had provided was unbathroomed and twenty yards from the cheerless hole where a rusty geyser had almost worn away the metal below by constant dripping. It was cleanish by English standards, but the plug would not fit. The Chief Inspector left in a bad temper, not improved by the sight of Sergeant Honeybody's great red face and the smell of kippered herrings.

He did not enquire after the Sergeant's health, but Honeybody, who laboured under the delusion that the world was interested in his entrails, volunteered the information that he was fit but gone in the hams and could undertake light duties.

The Chief Inspector glowered and toyed with porridge and cream and was wondering dismally about bacon and eggs when the waitress gave him an envelope.

"They bloody well give you the bill before the food's into you," he said. "Hallo, look at this."

The writing was rather spidery, but very legible. It said, curtly, "Dear Chief Inspector, as I gather you are investigating the death of a Mr. Title, you may wish to interview me as he called here. I shall be at home between ten and ten thirty, but then will depart on business. Yours faithfully, Hugh Palabras."

"The Vicar told him," said Honeybody through a kippered aroma.

"Or the publican. I don't like it!"

"He might serve a drop of Madeira in the middle of the morning, some of them still do, with a bit of seed cake. Very comforting, I always find it."

"Oh, we'll see him, but first the landlord."

"A funny cuss," said the Sergeant. "A widower and if there are women in his life they are away from the village and even the market town, Granchester. Around fifty, I'd reckon, and looks as though he's done a bit of work in the Ring in his time. One of his ears is thickened and his nose is flattened a bit."

He must have got that from the barmaid, ruminated the Chief Inspector sourly, pumping her between dalliance as it were. He said: "Check with the licensing police. They'll have his record back to his birth." He settled on devilled kidneys while the Sergeant "thought he would toy with another kipper".

"He doesn't mix too well for a publican," said Honeybody later as they tapped at the door of Bosky Lane's minuscule office, with its desk stacked high with papers.

"Bloody bumf," growled Lane as they crowded into the room. "Two hours a day keeps my head just above water, and the auditor comes in this afternoon. So short and sweet, my hearties, if you please."

"Death is important, too," said Harry mildly.

"But why did the bastard have to do it in my effing hotel?"

"Anybody could have doctored the brandy bottle," said Harry, "though only his prints turned up on it. Of course, kids in nursery school wear gloves when they are rifling teacher's purse, thanks to the thriller writers."

"He locked the door on himself and took his life," said Lane.

"Looks very like but what niggles is that there was no note. Ninety-eight point something of suicides either write notes or give blatant indication of their intent, such as capering on high window sills, the exception generally being customers who impulsively fling themselves under trains."

"I told you that he was mouse quiet while he was here.

In view of his previous gabbing it may be that he was turned in and brooding."

"What did you make of Miss Higgins?" asked the Chief Inspector abruptly.

"Make? Nothing! We get scores of those smart young cows staying. She might be a whore on holiday—they do take holidays—or be a demonstrator round the supers. Scores of 'em!"

"So she goes and gets knocked down outside your door."

"Ah! Somebody gets off the main road, has a few gins—though not here because I watch it like a hawk—tears through the village and side-swipes her. She was sober. Her order was one glass of Beaujolais with pâté and then game pie, plus a Cointreau with coffee, which she didn't finish. It would not have made a curate tight or one of your ruddy analysis machines blush."

"Did you tell Sir Hugh Palabras I was here?"

"You're joking! Sir Hugh sits next to the Judge at the Assizes if he wants to, the Chief Constable is always sipping port from his famous cellars and he bloody well owns the county. Why should I have to tell him things about two nasty little London lackeys from the Incapable Criminal Investigation Dept.?"

Lane's powerful torso had risen above his chair. A very tough customer, thought Harry.

"No need to be rude," he said.

"You haven't even tried me yet. Now run along."

"Thank you for your co-operation," said Harry as they went out. Closing the door, he said to the Sergeant, "Note the change in atmosphere, which means that he has the assurance that somebody with the necessary clout will stand by him. Sir Hugh, I presume. I will be interested to see that old patrician."

"Should be paediatrician judging by the number of by-blows they say he's studded," remarked Honeybody with what Harry thought to be a certain amount of that envy which men reserve for their fellows who achieve large illegitimate families.

Harry drove the car for the quarter of a mile involved. He would have preferred to walk, the morning was fine and sunny and those birds which had so far escaped the Vicar were twittering. He thought of Sir Hugh, the intellectually brilliant student with fearsome wealth—his father had been fatally mauled by a tiger when he was eighteen—who had captured a Parliamentary seat at twenty-two, been groomed for an under-secretaryship, changed parties twice, and over the years relapsed into the eccentricity with which he was dubbed. Churchill had liked to dagger him. "An undecided fascist or communist but of course in a genteel way" : "the bras, one is afraid, frames a womanish temperament". Palabras had never really recovered, but had retreated into the eighteenth century : the by-blows, many achieving high rank with the B.B.C. or in the T.V. industry, were legendary. They said Palabras had fathered one hundred and eighteen, thereby beating the English record previously held by a venerable white-haired painter who had died from his labours.

An old rogue elephant, thought the Chief Inspector, with some kind of vague mystique and always the thought that England might turn to him were the emergency dire enough. And not the only one, the place was a kind of sink for old blokes with panaceas and always had been from Charlie Marx and before. The Palabras pile had been described in the briefing : in spite of their elderly baronetcy, the Palabras had come into full fig about 1840 when the Derbyshire coal mine had started to produce black gold and give the local peasantry tuberculosis. The Palabras incumbent of the day had occupied thirty fairly modest acres, but upon this he had erected a mansion of hideous aspect, with a generally Grecian character about it. With their perversity, the four subsequent generations had cherished it. Sir Hugh had installed American bathrooms and air conditioning, but from the outside it made the blood run cold. The nineteenth century had run to nerve-racking eccentricity, thought Harry as he paused to park his car in the drive.

"A cosy crib," said Honeybody. "Electric blankets and hot ladies, I'll bet. You can't beat the old aristocracy when it comes to the old comfort. And the wine cellar: I'd like to have a few hours in *that*."

They had perhaps kept the house because of the gardens, reasoned Harry. Started in the seventeenth century, continued according to the individual taste of the reigning Palabras, they were only now reaching a magnificent prime. If you ignored the house, the vista delighted in every direction. It must cost a fortune to keep up, and Sir Hugh charged nothing to the public who were allowed in on the last Sunday in the month.

The youngish, deadpan butler who opened the door was expecting them and as sometimes depicted in the Sunday supplements when news was slow, Sir Hugh sat in his workroom—he forbade use of the word 'study'—with his portrait by John behind him. The broadness of his shoulders made him look shorter than his five feet ten. His wrinkled, rather puckish face was surmounted by a mane of curly white hair, overflowing around his collar. One rather expected blue eyes, but they were smallish and black and Harry remembered that the original Palabras had been a Spanish Jew employed by Walsingham as a translator and interpreter. The blood had survived, though Sir Hugh was himself a fervent anti-semite, attributing to the Jews the strange combination of both communism and grasping capitalism.

He rose and gave his eager smile. "Chief Inspector and Sergeant, is it not? Welcome to Firbank, an ugly old thing but my own. It grows on you. Sit ye down. We have half an hour."

"How did you know we were down?" asked Harry.

Sir Hugh consulted his watch. "I always have a bit of cake and a drop of Madeira at this hour. Perhaps you'll join me." Without waiting for assent, he reached up and jerked the silken bell-pull. "Know? The Chief Constable is an old friend. I thought that as this poor fellow Title had visited me, you would want to call but perhaps experience a certain trepidation in pestering a wealthy old fellow of notoriously evil temper. So hence the invite."

"It was kind of you. We don't think there is much to the death of Justin Title except that it does not conform to a pattern, and we go largely by patterns because people run to form, and suicide was not Title's form. He was a man of dubious pursuits, by the way."

"A criminal?"

"No convictions but an associate of criminals and a very glib man indeed who chased the quick buck."

Sir Hugh had the habit of polishing his nose with the bowl of his pipe and he did this while a small maid served wine and pieces of seed cake. Honeybody scarcely disguised his drooling, whether for wine, cake or maid Harry felt undecided. It was probably a combination of all three. The girl's eye momentarily met Harry's and he remembered the under parlourmaid planted in the house by M.I.5. What was her name? Stinting he recalled.

"Thank you, Stinting," said Sir Hugh at that moment.

Looks sweet seventeen, thought Harry, but probably an

experienced thirty. Most people in Intelligence, and curiously enough crime, looked younger than their age.

"Over the years," said Sir Hugh as she departed, "my family have accumulated a lot of priceless bric-a-brac. We have one of the few El Grecos outside Spain and a poor Titian in good physical condition. In 1860 Sir Alaric bought up the largest private collection of Reynolds. Say two million on the auction block, possibly five million if the Picassos my father bought in 'twenty-four fetch the expected price. Title was trying to flog burglar alarms."

"As a matter of interest, are you insured?"

Sir Hugh gave his attractive grin. He was a charmer, thought Harry.

"I leave business to the Estate managers, six of 'em with umpteen clerks and typists. But I put my foot down against insurance. I do not believe in mad American millionaires gloating in secret over stolen canvasses. If they were pinched it would be a ransom job—fifty thousands pounds and no questions asked. It would be much better for me to pay up than to foot the quoted premium. But I can see," he twinkled, "you consider that compounding a felony. Of course it's done every day in a respectable way!"

"Did he want to see round the house?"

"I had him shown by my secretary, Miss Drinkwater. No harm in getting a free opinion, though we have the latest alarms installed."

"He made a good free estimate of burglar possibilities and apparently did not think too much of your system. And I gather that all servants except one sleep out."

"I don't want servants hanging around perpetually," said Sir Hugh. "It was a nasty nineteenth-century concept put up by cads. My own suite is separate and at nights is kept locked. In it are kept the twelve most valuable paintings, the Cellini bowl, etcetera. I suppose a pack of maidservants would be unlikely to repel a gang of competent thieves: more likely to be in league with 'em. I keep a loaded shotgun in my suite and at night my dog sleeps against my bedroom wall."

The Chief Inspector had been conscious of a slight woolly odour which he had attributed to Sir Hugh's Harris tweeds, but now he saw a pair of unpleasant green eyes in one corner of the room. It was a formidable dog and probably short-tempered.

"If I said the word he'd tear your throat out," said Sir Hugh.

"I dare say he has more respect for the laws of England to which you so often refer in your speeches."

Sir Hugh chuckled. "I see they briefed you very well. It would be Quarles I suppose."

Harry felt limp. "I don't know any Quarles."

"I don't advise you to, Chief Inspector. He is mean in the American sense of the word. I knew him during the war when he was in Special Services. But taking you at face value, I will tell you about Title. He was pleasant and businesslike. I first had the feeling that he might have been employed by the Mr. Quarles you know naught of, but I happen to know the firm he had the credentials from and they are certainly exactly what they purport to be. His eyes roved. He spotted a safe I have concealed behind that little Dutch painting over there. I was watching him and saw his face, muscle-reading being one of my hobbies. It did not matter: I put it down to professional astuteness and the fact that he was an advance man for a gang of burglars, as you seem to intimate, did not occur to me. It did not seem, on reflection, that he was anything more than a go-getting salesman.

"However, he did ask about the other people. I should explain that dotted around the Estate are four largish houses.

It has been a family tradition, dating back two hundred years, to let them to, we will say, deserving people in whom the Palabras family are interested. The leases are not excessive and in the old days this part of the world was so dull that it suited the Family to have good company nearby. Sheridan spent a year here and m'grandfather angled unsuccessfully for Shaw in 1890. They are not poor people. Old General Gould has a priceless collection of pearls his ancestors looted from unfortunate natives. Señor Abajo has his collection of gold Spanish coins, Miss Sloper, who has a one-hundred-year lease granted to her great-aunt for favours rendered to my father, a foolish man one is afraid when it came to sex, possesses a nice collection of water colours. Title was interested or so I thought. Whether he called on 'em or not I don't know."

"If you are surveying an estate for reasons of burglary, you also survey the near neighbours," said Harry. "In making a getaway one would not wish to bang into either old generals or maiden ladies."

Sir Hugh's small eyes half shut for a long second. "I hadn't thought of that. To be practical what should I do?"

"Hire a couple of night-watchmen and install an alarm to the local police station: get two more dogs for outside work."

"I don't want men hanging around and Bonzo would go for a strange dog on sight."

"Then get an independent assessor to make suggestions regarding alarms. Here," he scrawled a name on one of his visiting cards, "this bloke is supposedly the best there is."

"I am in your debt," declared Sir Hugh rather grandly. "I must, I am afraid, leave now, but I can place you in the capable hands of Miss Drinkwater. She is less of a secretary, by the way, than a P.R.O. She has my full confidence. Perhaps you will accompany me."

He locked the door of his study as they came out. Harry saw that he had a housekeeper-like key chain affixed to the top button of his fly.

Though he greeted her casually, Harry had known Miss Joan Drinkwater for seven years, as a Fleet Street journalist, flack, political reporter, and writer on cookery. Forty-ish, fairish and thin. An intelligent woman. Of her private life he had no idea except that she liked brandy-and-soda as a drink.

"I must be running," said Sir Hugh, at the door of her office down the hall. "This is Chief Inspector James and Sergeant Uh. Show them anything they want—within reason of course. Well it's been nice to meet you."

"You have your notes?" asked the lady.

"They are in the car, Miss Drinkwater." Sir Hugh trundled himself away.

"What are you doing here, Joan?" asked Harry as he pecked her cheek. "In this gallery as the frogs say."

"Money. It pays well, and the husband is an engineer in a local works. We were sick of London. Old Hugh is an amiable old relic. I do the research for his speeches, sub his articles, tout for speaking engagements—he still peddles the stuff very well. What snoopeth thou for?"

"Man named Justin Title took poison at the pub and my superiors are dubious whether he fell or was pushed."

The lines in her face came out. "You, Sergeant Honeybody *and* a pub is incredible. I showed Title round on Sir's instruction. Very smarmy, very sweet and called me 'dear lady' until I could have kneed him. Crook?"

"Entrepreneur-like, setting up jobs and fronting. No record, but no reason to shuffle off at all that I can see. He was up to something without a doubt. It's a puzzle."

"As a professional asker of questions, I admired Title. He kept on and on in quite a subtle way. There is, of course, a lot of valuable stuff here. When Sir Hugh was away last year I amused myself by taking an inventory. There was some seventeenth-century stuff, knives mostly, that he didn't even know about. I got an expert down and I guess we unearthed thirty thousand quid's worth of stuff including a small Etty in the attics."

"You have that much authority?"

"He is no piker. I run the place. He does not have to worry about appointments or air tickets. I can roughly do what I like on the business side."

"The servants except the valet live out, one understands."

"They have various cottages around the village. You know he's an old ram, six times co-respondent at a total cost of some fifty thousand pounds. Nowadays he prefers to be without witnesses to his importunities, to coin a phrase. What the butler saw is strictly out at Firbank. But are you intimating that Title was murdered because of something that happened here?"

"Thieves fall out. Maybe this was a juicy plum and another thief thought he could eliminate Title and take over the operation."

"Do you want to see the house?"

"No, Joan, there is no point to it. I advised your boss to get a professional adviser on burglary-proofing. I'd like to see around the Estate."

"We might as well go now." She looked at her watch. "My husband eats in the canteen: I eat at the pub so it might as well be on your expense account."

"Do we walk?"

"A car is best: you can't see the roads because of the landscaping. They are narrow because they were originally designed for small horse carriages but they do the job."

"Guide me, please," said Harry as they got in the car, Honeybody's weight making the back seat groan slightly.

"I must tell you that these houses are four in number and were let by Sir Hugh's father. Hugh does not like the tenants particularly. He thinks old General Gould was rather the most incompetent British general ever, if possible, tolerates Miss Sloper whom he refers to as a 'meddlesome old bitch' because of her charitable activities, cannot understand old Señor Abajo, who is ninety-three, and of course loathes dear Bruggles, the fourth tenant, last heard of filming in Spain."

Bruggles, thought Harry dismally, the pet name for the stateliest homo of the English stage, which was saying something. Knighted and sixty-five, Bruggles had the reputation of not understanding the words, generally Shakespearian, that he declaimed in his perfect voice, but his looks were perennial and the expressiveness of his eyes made him perfect for film and T.V. At least you could count him out, Harry supposed.

"This Abajo," he said. "A Spaniard, one supposes?"

"The last of the Castrati," said Miss Drinkwater.

Harry eased the car still slower. "Did I hear you say . . . ?"

"In the nineties," she said, "there was still feudal magnificence in Spain, Montague and Capulet stuff included. One Duke was very fond of seventeenth-century church music. His counter tenor upped and died and you know that they are as scarce as hens' teeth. He was walking along under the wistaria vines when he heard an eleven-year-old boy singing like an angel." She shrugged. "He had three resident physicians, the boy's parents were willing—they worked about the *hacienda* and had no choice—and so Señor Abajo's voice is unchanged, though it is a little piping sound now. He got a magnificent musical education and the Duke left him ninety thousand pounds in 1927."

"He can't live alone," said Harry.

"There are two daily women. Servants are no problem on the Estate, Sir Hugh seeing to that, and he has a manservant, a surly sort known as Chef Beedle."

"Chef?"

"He has a French qualification and a framed certificate in his kitchen to substantiate it. I am told he cooks like an angel, Señor Abajo only liking Spanish food. Here we are, by the way."

It was a two-storey, pleasant Victorian house, with a tiny garden filled with rose trees. A brass plate read '*Los Rosales*'.

"He insists on being addressed as 'chef'," said Miss Drinkwater as they rang the bell.

He was short, black-avised with side-whiskers, and with an expression of unpleasant pomposity.

"Chef Beedle, I presume," said Harry, feeling he was in darkest Africa. "We, the two of us, are from Scotland Yard, investigating the death of one Justin Title. Could we see Señor Abajo?"

"He is awake at the moment," said Chef Beedle, evidently pleased at the bestowal of the name, "and he did see Mr. Title, but you must not tire him. I should be present, but do not take too long because I am seething his testicles in champagne."

As his wife often forecast it had come at last, thought the Chief Inspector, the ruin of the neural channels caused by overwork and excessive drinking. Every year some inspector or other was quietly taken away and not heard of again. But then he saw Honeybody's vast belly swelling, a sure sign of indignation.

"What did you say?"

"The Spanish can't get enough of them, sir. Of course statistically it is difficult, but I have an arrangement with a friendly slaughterhouse man at Granchester. Three lovely ones I procured yesterday and the secret is the amount of cumin in the sauce. Slice thinly, seethe in champagne, egg and breadcrumb, deep fry, prepare a white sauce..." Chef Beedle's eyes glinted behind his thick glasses.

"I'd like to try a spoonful," said Honeybody, placated.

"So you shall, in twenty minutes' time when the Señor eats." Chef Beedle recognised a kindred spirit. "And Señor Abajo has a supply of Montilla sent to him by old admirers, him singing up to the age of eighty-five, which goes well with *criadillas* but the old gent is forbidden alcohol so he is liberal with visitors."

They entered the hall, furnished in the Spanish way with inept little gilt chairs upon which human loins had never rested, and progressed into a large room, the drapes of the windows three-quarters closed. Señor Abajo was a wizened little brown nut of a man, with a tiny bell-like voice, who apologised for not arising from his wicker couch.

"In fact I cannot unless Chef Beedle does the lifting." His English was accentless.

"They have twenty minutes before the *criadillas* are ready, Señor Abajo."

A tiny tongue caressed the Señor's wrinkled lips. "When one gets old one thinks of life as a progression of meals revolving around Chef Beedle. Friends, and to have friends at my time of life is incredible, send the old man delicacies and thank God my digestion remains unimpaired. However, to your business. This man, Title, was selling burglar alarms. I have some gold coins, perhaps seventeen thousand pounds' worth, which are in a locked cabinet. There is insurance, however: it is excessive because I look at them sometimes and do not wish to let them moulder in some banker's vault. Having seen many rogues in my time I thought he was one. Poison, so Chef Beedle told me the village was saying. What was it?"

"Barbiturates."

"They did not have them in my day. I used arsenic on my *padrone,* the Duke."

Honeybody's dentures jerked as they did when he was under nervous stress.

Chef Beedle wagged his head in admonishment.

"It was a fair exchange for what he did to me. I waited thirty years and then some new American weed-killer came on the market..." the old gentleman's eyes closed and he drifted into the sweet sleep of old age.

"The old gent has a sense of humour, I think," said Chef Beedle, albeit doubtfully. "Better come into the kitchen, and let him be. He only naps about fifteen minutes at a time."

"Been with him long?" asked Harry as they entered the large, glittering kitchen, over which Miss Drinkwater purred appreciatively. There was a large certificate, as Miss Drinkwater had said, advertising the Chef's merit and issued from a former French colony. Beedle poured out four large glasses of Montilla from a black bottle. "Comes from a little village outside Cordoba," he said, "and is lighter than sherry, which is its imitator."

Honeybody was already dipping his nose into the bouquet while Beedle did things on top of the Aga cooker. "I've been here eight months," he grunted without turning. "I was in Lisbon working at the Coq d'Or when I saw an ad in the *Sunday Times.*"

"You speak excellent English."

"My father was an Afro who worked for ten years in Cardiff, my mum was French." There was a hiss of deep frying.

"I suppose Title was a complete stranger to you?"

"Only saw him the once: like the old gent said he was a greasy article what you wouldn't trust with anything. You get to know them in the restaurant trade and when I was young I waited in some ripe old places. Here, sit at the table, and I'll give you a saucerful. It's beautiful, but however he kids himself the old gent only eats a morsel at a time, and then his guts rumble like the B.B.C.'s African Service."

"Not for me," shuddered Miss Drinkwater.

"With the world half starved you turn your nose up at good food. Ever tried sheeps' eyeballs or cows' teats done in sherry?"

"I don't like to think of it!"

"If people did their own slaughtering there'd be more vegetarians. Ever had chitterlings? Or haggis, come to that. Here we are! Eat it while it's hot. I'll put the old gent's morsel out to rest."

It was delicious, decided Harry, but could he persuade his wife...? "Disgusting," she would say and clamp her lips together in the way which became more formidable with each year of marriage.

"Joan," said Harry as they drove away, "how come you knew the Chef had his certificate displayed in his kitchen?"

"Good God, what minds you have! Old Abajo still has business letters and once a month I come over, have a Montilla with him, and take any letters back to answer, pay the cheques into his account, etcetera. He owns three quite modern blocks of apartments in the London area and some stock in French companies. I would consider him well off."

"Lady Bountiful, eh?"

"Come off it." Miss Drinkwater coloured.

"At least he seems to prefer other things to soup. We'll see General Gould next, perhaps."

"He lives with a niece." She shrugged. "You can form your own opinion of the lady, who is a Conservative candidate *manqué,* but old Gould is shrewd enough. The kennels are over in Granchester. No doubt he was daft professionally —his Army fled successively from Italians, Japs, Jews and finally Egyptians or something of that nature—but when it comes to his personal affairs you can't diddle him. I say old, but he's only seventy and there was some talk of putting him in charge in Northern Ireland. His Military Cross came when he was with the Black and Tans as a youth and he considers himself an expert on that part of the world."

"How the hell was he given the lease?"

"Sir Hugh's father thought he was the kind of man England wanted. That was many years before he lost his way going back to Dunkirk and they had to fly him out of the country and send him to Africa, I suppose to get him out of the way. Sir Hugh thinks his trouble is that he can't read maps. His hounds are always taking the wrong turning and bailing up people in outside closets. Here we are."

It was almost a facsimile of Señor Abajo's house, but the cunning landscaping produced the illusion of aloneness. Birds twittered in a manner which would convulse the Vicar with envy, and what was clearly a retired N.C.O. with a waxed moustache answered the door.

There were various North African animals represented by their heads. If the General had failed to bag Italians he had evidently run wild among their game, even down to camel rugs and some small crucifixes filched out of churches. Introduced by Miss Drinkwater, Honeybody leering round in quest of a cask of chianti—or so Harry sourly assumed—the General was frankly a shifty type. Uniform probably gave him dignity, but in slacks and tee-shirt, a trowel in his hand, one noticed the close-set evasive eyes, side-long glances and evident intention of locking himself in the loo in cases of emergency. Ordered to advance by the General, Harry decided that he would personally have scampered the other way.

"M'niece, Mrs. Peremely-Fox," had muttered Gould, as though he was selling this stout, thin-mouthed lady with the black wig. "A cup of tea," he had ordered the manservant as Honeybody's jaw dropped.

Harry thought that even in Australia tea was not taken a scant half-hour before lunch, but he soon knew the reason as he tasted the thin brew, diluted with a dob of evaporated milk: the General and Mrs. Peremely-Fox did not believe in wasting good money on servants, public or otherwise. In the short time which elapsed between its ordering and production—a disused petrol can of the stuff probably perennially simmered on the stove—Mrs. Peremely-Fox grasped the subject of capital punishment. "Don't you think the cat should be recalled?" she asked Honeybody, whom lack of noon alcohol was causing to look faintly brutal.

"And whipping, ma'am," agreed the Sergeant. "The birch being a rare detergent."

(You could never tell, thought Harry, which of Honeybody's malapropisms were intentional.)

"I suppose you've seen it done on many occasions?" Mrs. Peremely-Fox moistened her lips.

"Many a time I've administered the cat," lied Honeybody affably. "The art is not to cut down to the bone or the chaplain objects, they not liking the sight of the gore on account of Gentle Jesus. The birch is a different kettle of fish, applied direct to the buttocks: rare bruising it causes if I may say so without offence, and the chaplains approved."

"And hangings, I suppose you saw many before the lily-livered lot abolished the last protection that a virtuous woman has?"

"Seventeen," fabricated Honeybody, "including once when the head came off and two when I had to mount a step-ladder in order to swing on the ankles as an act of Christian charity."

Mrs. Peremely-Fox looked about to faint from ecstasy. "I once told Sir Alec," she muttered, but the General intervened. "The firing squad is a clean death. Seven men I had to place before one for cowardice in the face of the enemy. Incidentally even in those days their hair was over regulation length. The Americans only shot one of theirs, and I told Winston that was the obvious sign of their inferiority though they seem to have bucked up a bit in Vietnam and hit the wogs for six."

"A certain Mr. Title," fairly bleated Harry "who came round last week, was found poisoned at the pub. We understand he saw you."

"Burglar alarms," snorted Gould, "and that to a man like me who spent his career in the field. I am licensed to possess a revolver, and a selection of shotguns. My man, Bottomley, was an R.S.M. in charge of rifle instruction and he sleeps in the house. An intruder would get short shrift, I assure you."

"If only Edward would reinstate the lash," whined Mrs. Peremely-Fox. "It would be the making of him, I'm sure."

General Gould's sly eyes showed a touch of impatience as he glanced at his watch. "We lunch in exactly twelve minutes," he said. "This fellow Title, I got rid of him speedily. Told him not to be a bloody fool. One of my boys was staying here for a few days and he agreed with me."

On the mantelpiece were photographs of three large, youngish men in naval uniform. Harry recognised one as a Commander who had thrice run his destroyer aground: an old Service family, this.

"Do you got out at night much, sir?" he asked.

The General's eyes rotated round the room and his mouth pursed around yellow teeth. "Expertise, I suppose. This fellow Title did ask me that. I told him truthfully, 'No, very little'. Once the hounds are taken back to kennel on hunting days I take my bit of dinner and settle down to writing my autobiography, 'Hitting Them For Six'. When there's no sport it's a bit of rough shootin'—we have a few hares and rabbits—potterin' in the garden and early to bed. Don't suppose I go out five times over a year. Attended too many goddamned smoked-salmon parties with the politicos when I was working. Title, hrmph, poisoned himself, didn't he? Unusual for an Irishman. They make splendid material if you see they do take the weekly shower and keep drink away from them."

"He might have been murdered."

"A lot of Irishmen are murdered," said the General, "that would explain it. But now, sir, it is my rule never to let good food get cold, prices being what they are."

"Phew," said Honeybody, as they got outside, "I never wanted a drink so much, that tea fair curdling the colon."

"For once I agree with you," observed Miss Drinkwater. "You've no idea how mean he is. Exists on kedgeree and manages to make a profit out of the hounds. Miss Sloper lunches at the pub, so we could see her there."

It was market day over at Granchester, although a shadow of its former self. But tradition dies hard in the West Country and the farmers' wives came in to rummage in the three large supermarkets, their husbands in city suits arrived for a word with their accountant, bank manager and garage. The Welfare State had abolished the purveyors of cure-alls, but as Harry remembered there was always a little man selling a knife with which to cut corns and a small group of stalls carrying anything from material to battered tins of canned fruit. And there was still the smell of cattle dung, but this pervaded the very marrow of the old town. It was the thing for the wealthier farmers, business over at one, to drive over to the Marquis of Tenterton, which in the old days had put on a posh 'farmers' ordinary' to exclusively male company. So the Italian head waiter was able to assure them that in five minutes' time he would not have been able to book them in as his smooth, plump hand deftly palmed Harry's tip.

They decided to have a drink in the bar, where Miss Drinkwater assured them that Miss Sloper would be having a dry Martini. So she was and by daylight Harry placed her in the fifties but with magnificent skin and a very upright, lithe carriage. Probably a lady to be reckoned with!

John Drinkwater presented them.

"I saw you last night," Miss Sloper said in her husky voice as Harry ordered drinks. "Thanks, I will have another. That poor woman! I phoned the county hospital: slight concussion and a cracked cheekbone. Did they get the driver?"

"Not that I heard," said Harry. "They probably will not. It happens all the time . . . if it was an accident."

"Do you mean it was deliberate, but then for God's sake why? I signed a statement this morning . . . I mean I suppose it could have been deliberate but I thought it criminal or drunken driving."

"Miss Sloper," said Harry "did you hear a car start up as Miss Higgins came to her own car?"

Her eyes were cold and oddly knowing. "Now you mention it I believe I did, but as to swearing . . ."

"It has been known," said Harry, "for a driver to lie in wait, as it were, for his victim. An American gangster ploy. They usually cut the engine because a parked car with the motor running attracts notice."

Miss Drinkwater gave a little shudder as she lifted her gin. "I hardly think we have American gangsters here, or indeed any Americans except the tourists whom the locals merely rob, not murder."

"Some good cribs to crack, Joan! Miss Sloper, did you see a man named Title?"

"Oh, yes, greasy article but these speciality salesmen sometimes are. Yet he talked sense and ninety per cent persuaded me. I asked him for a quote."

"And therefore gave him the run of the house!"

"You mean that he was casing the joint as one believes the saying is? I'm damned... but he poisoned himself, didn't he?"

"He took poison in brandy."

"What poison?"

Nosy, thought Harry, or something. "A mixture of barbiturates," he replied. "Do you write detective novels, Miss Sloper? One of those gentle English ladies who write so fearsomely?"

"Just a general reader. No, I was wondering because poison is not easy to get, except insecticides, and nobody wants to consider himself an insect. I live alone except for an elderly housekeeper and quite often eat here, old Gladys subsisting almost solely on toasted cheese and stout. Now you mention it, Title was a trifle over curious about my comings and goings."

"Let us have one more, and pray, Miss Sloper, have lunch on the Government, a rare experience for those out of the nick." From the corner of his eye he noted that Honeybody had vanished.

Miss Sloper looked slyly amused. "Thank you, Mr. James, I will gladly accept free skilly and boiled bacon, or has the Welfare State changed it to hygienic cornflakes and ham?"

"The old formula plus minced meat and T.V. the last time I saw them slopping it on to the tin plates. We think that Title was in fact casing Sir Hugh's. The man scarcely wots what he has. It would be necessary to know the pattern of the other residents of the enclave for getaway purposes."

"Hugh is an odd character," said Miss Sloper. "To complete his eighteenth-century bit you would think he would have twenty-seven legitimate children, imposed on three dead wives, and all the girls married into the more ancient peerages, the boys double-crossing New Zealand, etcetera."

"He could never risk a son who might challenge and outshine him," said Miss Drinkwater, "yet he is a good fellow as long as he thinks he is sole cock on his dunghill—not that it is anything but a luxurious dunghill, *coq de luxe* you might say."

"The heir," observed Miss Sloper, "is a pallid second cousin, much younger, who farms unsuccessfully in Norfolk. I met him once."

Harry wondered irritably where Honeybody was and eventually shepherded the ladies to the dining-room, conscious of the gaze of Bosky Lane through a hatchway near the serving entrance. To his surprise, the Sergeant, seated with a napkin tucked into the top of his waistcoat, rose like a whale at the sight of a harpooner. "A bit of business called me away. Sit down, ladies, and the chef himself told me the soles are gorgeous, done with ham and skinned white grapes." He bustled round. For some reason his charms, gross as they are, strike some chord with the ladies and both Miss Drinkwater and her friend appeared delighted to be seated by him.

So in the end it was Honeybody who in fact ordered the kidney soup and the soles, rather to the Chief Inspector's chagrin. He had set his mind on steak-and-oyster pudding, but there was no gainsaying Honeybody when he had the menu between his teeth, as it were. But there was something exciting the Sergeant, Harry knew by experience, so he slipped an antacid tablet in his mouth and braced himself for pangs of dyspepsia.

"Neither of you ladies had seen Title before?"

"No," said Miss Drinkwater, "and I never forget a face."

"I do forget faces," said Miss Sloper, "and once thought a respectable clergyman of my acquaintance was a fishmonger who supplied me with Dublin prawns: most embarrassing as I kept asking him if he preferred sea water for his crustaceans. He seemed to think I was pursuing an obscure theological point. But, no, I do not think I ever saw Title apart from his knocking on my door and delivering a good sales pitch. I must say that he seemed a most specious talker, the kind that can always turn over money if they keep off the drink."

Harry recognised the faint leer in Honeybody's eyes. In an hour the ladies departed, Miss Drinkwater on Sir Hugh's business, Miss Sloper on something to do with Girl Guides, with whom apparently the district proliferated.

Honeybody broke down all Harry's defences by announcing that he would pay for a port. He had private means in the shape of a raw-boned wife who ran a fish-and-chip shop in defiance of Police Regulations.

"I had a gander at the public bar; my friend the barlady tipped me off that one Percy Ockers might have some information. He looks like a shrivelled apple on legs. He's dodgy, I guess on social security plus all the lurks. An entrepreneur is the classy word for it. He wanted to know about the chances of fifteen quid, ten for him and five for a friend named Dirty Douglas. Years of study and self-denial," proclaimed the Sergeant relishing a final mouthful of port mixed with Stilton cheese, "makes me think there might be pay dirt, this fellow Ockers obviously being willing to sell anybody or anything."

"Any idea what he may have?"

"Nothing. I told him it would be five pound down on spec and the balance if he came through."

"He doesn't sound a good witness, and by inference and name Dirty Douglas doesn't. 'Me Lord and gentlemen of the Jury I present one Dirty Douglas!'" Stilton always made the Chief Inspector sour.

"We couldn't put either of them in the box anyway," soothed Honeybody, "because it would be obvious to the feeblest jury they were doing it for lolly. We haven't been paying out much lately, so why not sport the fifteen and argue with Accounts later?"

This sort of payment was one of the most ticklish parts of the job: though paid informers produced most of the convictions the lily-white British public, whining about the rate of burglary, were always prepared to throw their arms up in horror when it was mentioned. So Harry deliberated through his coffee, but finally shrugged his shoulders. "Where do we see these ginks?"

"We just walk casual-like into the public bar in five minutes' time." He ignored his superior's baleful look.

Percy Ockers was red-faced and apple-like, giving the slight impression of being worm-eaten. Dirty Douglas was tall, thin and had immensely long arms. He had obviously rarely washed since his mum quit the task. Huddled with them and Honeybody in one corner, trying to get to the windward of Douglas, Harry ordered a round of double whiskies.

Percy Ockers was a man who came to the point quickly. After palming the fiver he said, "There's a local layin'-off ground named Dodger's Acre. It's flat but unused with a lot of bushes dotted around. You can drive a car on it right off the main road, goin' cautious-like because you might run over a couple of bodies. It's mostly the backs of the cars, though."

Harry was momentarily bemused, but then said, "I see."

"A powerful lot you do see in Dodger's Acre," said Dirty Douglas in his reedy little voice. "Disgustin'."

"Getting over a difficult 'urdle," said his mate, "on balmy nights they keep the windows open, it being' hot work as you gentlemen must well know—if in the state o' matrimony," he added as Harry glared at him. "And on the front seats of the car is placed clothing, coats with wallets in them, ladies' 'and bags and even umbrellas. So Douglas . . . well now, he makes his living at it, being quick and with long arms like a bleeding crane."

"It's God's judgment on 'em," said Douglas hastily, "me bein' the 'umble hinstrument of the Lord."

"Get to the point," snarled Harry.

"There's a knack in it," asserted Douglas, "it's not an easy lurk. You have to be long in the arm and fast on the hooves and be able to hear well. Then, p'raps you sing out 'Police here', petrifying the bloke as it can sometimes do, or, more risky because of orphings, 'Wot are you doin' to my daughter?' which is also petrifying. It's an art, sir, and no mistake about it."

"Douglas's dad brought him up to it," said Mr. Ockers. "And the dad was in it forty year, less the Second World War. Lor', he could remember 'orses and traps, a risky business until he found you could feed the animal lumps of sugar soaked in rum and make it pissed. Now, Douglas, what happened las' Thursday night?"

"Trade's falling off as the nights get nippy and they don't open the windows: unhealthy I call it, having raised six, all on Public Assistance and not a window in the bedroom since the Jerries blew them out in 1943. But I was lurkin', you never can tell and I know every blooming bush and tree. There was a flash article staying at the pub. It's my business and Percy's . . ."

"Leave me out of it," said Ockers.

"Well, say my business is to size up visitors to see whether a penny can be turned. I buy pheasants over at Granchester and sell 'em for double as being poached. The wickedness of the 'uming 'eart! The flash bloke was named Title and he was up to no good, take it from me. I've seen them come and I've seen them go to Granchester Assizes. Educated, la-di-da types. But I thought I might lurk that evening and wasn't doin' any good: all lorries and the local pros who are a wake-up to such lurks. Then this flash bloke drove in. I gave him ten minutes to turn it on, timin' being one of the trade secrets, and crep' up on him. God Save the Queen, bless 'er, they are still in the front talkin'. The bint was saying, 'I haven't unlimited money to spend.' I nearly fell over, though I've 'eard the blokes on that line of country.

" 'It would be cheap at ten thousand,' he said. I thought it was the D.T.s catching up, but my pulse was all right. She laughed, and I said to myself, 'Duggie, you're out of your class', and scarpered."

"Did you recognise the lady?" asked Harry.

"That's exactly what we 'ave to sell," said Ockers and the Chief Inspector slid two more notes out of his wallet.

"Ta," said Ockers. "It was Lady Bountiful wot runs the good works, never a pensioner with the piles without her pestering 'im. Striding along with the Girl Guides and 'itting me over the head with her shooting stick when I was giving a bit of the old curry to my dog. Dogs 'ave to be 'it as I told her. A certain Miss Sloper wot is a proper old bitch was in that car, as thick as thieves with this bloke. It's a puzzler to me: paying 'im a fiver is understandable, it being dark, but ten thousand—you wouldn't pay a handsome fillum star that."

"Thanks," said Harry, and left Honeybody behind.

Chapter Three

The Chief Inspector went out of the Marquis of Tenterton and phoned the Yard from a call box. There was a switchboard at the pub and he suspected the landlord might have sharp ears. He got on to Records, personified by a receiving tape machine. Nowadays they increasingly worked off tape or wire which could be erased as well as saving paper work. All documents in a case had to be kept at the disposal of the Defence, but Counsel could wear his jaw away demanding what had once been on tape. He itemised every person he had encountered in the case so far and asked for a complete run-down. It would then go to the computer which now managed Superintendent Hawker's own huge filing system, plus equally voluminous ones in the keeping of the Special Branch and M.I.5.

Then like all good policemen on assignment he took to his room to peruse his notes, a process which entailed the removal of his outer garments and shoes. His mouth felt sticky when Honeybody woke him up at six thirty.

"A tape from London, sent down by a driver—we've become important overnight."

Harry climbed into his clothes and got the pocket-size player out of his suitcase. Sitting on the bed beside Honeybody he plugged in the two sets of earphones and gave the stalwart Sergeant one.

An anonymous voice, possibly a drop-out from the B.B.C., counselled that the information was classified, must not be repeated to an unauthorised source, and that the tape was a debit against salary until officially returned.

Chef Beedle was thirty-nine and had been christened Christopher Aloysius by the Christian Fathers who laboured in his bit of Africa. Unlike British colonialism, with its culinary deserts, the French masters, with liberal use of the lash and thumbscrew, had weaned some of their faithful servitors from a natural inclination to cannibalism to a pretty high standard of Parisian cuisine and it was from one of these families that Chef Beedle sprang. He was a very good cook who had along the way become a Trotskyite. On Independence Day a warrant had been made out for his arrest, his compatriots much preferring the traditional comfort of bureaucratic corruption to Chef Beedle's spartan creed, so he had fled first to Algiers, secondly to Lisbon. A potentially dangerous man, opined M.I.5; an unbeliever in Democracy, the U.S.A., China and Russia, a combination which banished him from civilised society. But a good cook who could earn his sixty pounds a week at any Soho restaurant. It seemed surprising that he worked for Señor Abajo for sixteen pounds and his keep, though perhaps he had become fed up with restaurants.

Señor Abajo. Apart from not liking the Spanish regime and being friendly with such men as Picasso, said the voice disapprovingly, there was nothing against him. His operation was well known, but though deficient in certain ways he had been left a tidy fortune. He had been a serious musician whose recordings still earned him an income of two thousand a year. He was amiable, witty in a senile way, fairly active. It was unlikely that he should be active in the murdering way.

Sir Hugh. Perennially meddlesome, a man of money who could command his whim, which just lately was hatred of the Government. It was thought there was a chance of his becoming dangerous if certain contingencies eventuated, so said the voice turning professionally vague.

As the years rolled past, thought Harry, people and things became ever more distressingly complicated. He listened to the report on General Gould. Behind his façade of incompetence, the General was in some ways political. Recognising his shiftiness, politicians found a kindred spirit, so that after his graduation in the last place at Sandhurst, his military career had been swift. The fact was that though incredibly unsuccessful in the field, the General had had two great advantages: one, he employed brilliant but decayed journalists, with the rank of major, to explain away his losses: two, he was magnificent in defeat, crafty, venial when necessary, a master at dictating meaningless promises. In 1943 a section of Parliament came to the conclusion that he was the very man to deal with the Japanese, but he had been swiftly moved to the Middle East where he surrendered to the Russians in Persia, by mistake, the General not being good at languages. Harry gathered there was a bit of prejudice in the report, and that the old gentleman favoured Nationalist China from which he was suspected of receiving fifteen hundred pounds per year.

His niece, Mrs. Peremely-Fox, had been expelled from South Africa because she had denounced the Government as Communists who unduly favoured the black population, a community she was certain existed in the very desire to rape her. Mr. Peremely-Fox had run off in 1958 and was thought to be living in Valencia with a flamenco dancer. It was the lady's ambition to achieve parliamentary rank, but even with the General's not inconsiderable support the local committee still preferred a retired fishmonger.

There was a manservant, one Bottomley, of which the War Office could say only, somewhat gaspingly, that he had served the General for many years. He was a widower of fifty-four years and a former staff sergeant, reputed to be competent, of uncertain temper and possibly devoted to the General but more probably to his purse strings. His politics were unknown.

Of Miss Sloper little was known except that she had worked as an officer in the Second World War. Inheriting a considerable competence from an aunt, whose talent was mistressing wealthy old gents, the last being Sir Denville Palabras, father of Sir Hugh, she had settled as the local Lady Bountiful and busybody, the Girl Guides and old-age pensioners being her especial territory.

Miss Drinkwater possessed a good, but not particularly brilliant Fleet-Street record and was technically very competent in the mysteries of the profession. She lived at Granchester with her husband, a meek mechanical engineer who had a goodish job keeping the local sewerage plant turning over. But it was rumoured that Sir Hugh was to purchase one of the more ailing Sunday newspapers. 'The thinking man's Murdoch' was Sir Hugh's phrase in planning papers which specialised in politics and polemics rather than the more obvious pleasures of the lower classes. And, the recorded voice said, in accepting what might well be a boring kind of job, Miss Drinkwater would be on the inner track for an executive job with the new venture. The voice of Superintendent Hawker cut in: "And what better boost for the first numbers than the publication of those cursed papers?"

Harry dutifully erased the tape.

"I don't like the sound of either Beedle or Sloper," he said, "and come to that I do not really like anybody I've met here. What about that greasy landlord?"

"Simon Pure, but not Simple. Runs the pub well and does well for himself. Greasy, perhaps, but can be tough if necessary, and altogether the local boys like him. He's Sir Hugh's nominee and of course that counts for a lot, but there are a lot of decayed gentry around and he has a good way with them. An Irish background, but with not much accent as you will have noticed. Quite indifferent to politics, says the local sergeant, a Labour stalwart himself, and just makes the usual joking chatter about the parties. I would say he just likes a good life: wouldn't mind it myself with the best of food and drink, not that he drinks much during opening hours."

"I think we should cultivate Miss Sloper," said Harry.

"Doesn't like men terribly much!"

The Sergeant was pretty well infallible upon such subjects.

What did he know about Girl Guides except for one adolescent incident, thought Harry.

"I have an old aunt," leered Honeybody, "a certain lady who is head of the Girl Guides for quite a large area. The old bitch—my wife Dodo encouraging her for the sake of the Expectations, a cool twenty thousand if she has an accident and she's a mortal bad driver—but as I was saying perpetually drivelling on about the Guides so that I can remember bits of it. There are endless problems about the stoutness of their knickers, the young ladies preferring lightweight in the hot weather, but regulations specifying flannel or blue serge. I reckon I can find common ground with Miss Sloper if I put my mind to it. A convivial drink before dinner, a shared table, a good bottle or so and cunning questioning."

Oh, God, groaned Harry inwardly. He could not sustain his career without Honeybody, but this drunken incubus was perpetually involving them both in an alcoholic morass and he really did not often feel well in the morning these days. However, since he could think of little else to do, he acquiesced and it came to pass at seven forty-five that Honeybody's gross face was beaming at Miss Sloper. His great red smile always received a favourable response: Harry had worked it out that his helpmate was some kind of father figure in every woman's life, though why they coveted a Falstaffian dad he could not quite fathom.

"I hear you have Girl Guides, ma'am," said Honeybody, beckoning the barlady, "and I suppose you know my auntie, Flo Honeybody, from conferences, she being a great believer in its moral richness, so to speak, not that we find it in police work, all adolescents being little devils."

"Oh, I know your auntie," said Miss Sloper, accepting a pink gin, "always on about stouter knickers. I'm a bit in opposition to Auntie, but she is a prodigious worker for the movement. I suppose she must be sixty."

"Sixty-five."

"Does she still drive?" asked Miss Sloper dubiously.

"Against advice," said the Sergeant, his cheeks in mournful creases.

"I think it would be jolly if we joined tables," said Harry, manfully putting in his contribution, "it being very dull when you are away on a job."

Miss Sloper explained that she almost always dined by herself, fearing bores. Transient acquaintances were a different proposition.

In the event, Honeybody's cunning ploy came to little. The Sergeant did indeed know much about girl-guiding, but Miss Sloper knew more and blinded them with science. Getting a dozen whining teenagers up a Welsh mountain and cooking sausages over a bracken fire was routine to her. Broken ankles, snivelling colds, immoral advances by the peasantry she took in her stride.

But yet, thought Harry, Miss Sloper might be wearing a mask. Little tweaks of amusement, inward going, occasionally showed behind her cold eyes. Or was he imagining it? The woman could drink. The Chief Inspector nursed a small glass of wine throughout the meal which produced odd gurglings from his stomach, unused to dry food.

"Would you care to come back to my house for coffee and a liqueur?" asked Miss Sloper unexpectedly as Harry insisted on signing the bill.

"A lovely idea!" said Honeybody. "My auntie will be so pleased when I tell her."

"I gathered she was staunch teetotal, except for a little elder-flower wine for her stomach's sake. At least she harangues the girls to that purpose."

"A cupboard drinker," said Honeybody, probably lying. "Goes by the cupboard, inadvertently opens it, in a second has the sherry bottle uncorked, in another second has had a generous swig and closed the door, then goes back to pour out the Vicar's tea with a shaky hand."

"A worthy relative, one would imagine!" Miss Sloper commented.

The house was named the Elms, a tribute to respectability. They walked, Miss Sloper opining that she always found the half-mile good for the digestion. Honeybody's massive thews kept up with the lady's determined march without apparent effort, and he still burbled of girl-guidance under his moustache, but the Chief Inspector was breathless as they progressed down the narrow, discreetly lit laneways of Sir Hugh's Estate.

"My old girl retires to bed around eight, with her library book and whatever she thinks I won't notice missing out of the grog cupboard. I buy a line of cheap, bulk gin and leave a gill out for her each evening. It suits me to keep her." She opened the front door with a latch-key. The house smelled of furniture polish, and the living-room into which they were shown was a medley of tastes. The previous tenant had been chintzy nineteen-twentyish, and there were evidences of

Edwardian predecessors. Miss Sloper's tastes seemed to be basically Swedish. The effect was bizarre but on the comfortable side: in the corner was a small bar, a refrigerator and a coffee-making apparatus. Black coffee only, requested Harry, but Honeybody thought a drop of cherry brandy would go down well. Miss Sloper started the coffee and poured herself a brandy.

The light was rather gloomy as it shone out of the large picture window. "I'll pull the drapes," she said.

From where he was seated in a Windsor chair Harry first saw the star appear in the glass, a second before Miss Sloper first of all sat down, then slumped backwards so that they could see the hole between her eyes.

There was no sound of the shot, registered the Chief Inspector, but with a high-powered rifle there rarely was. "Get to the phone," he ordered Honeybody who was rapidly downing Miss Sloper's brandy.

Colliding with the gloomy hallstand, smelling of wet mackintoshes, he opened the front door. Something made a weird noise, a screech owl he decided. Otherwise there was only the sound of rustling tree branches and, far off, the noise of a car getting into high gear. He trotted aimlessly down the narrow roadway, turning left and right to peer into the trees.

There was somebody between the larches, reclining. A sniper? Aggression is the best police tactic and gives one a posthumous medal for gallantry, so Harry prepared to go into his notoriously ineffective rugby tackle which twenty years previously had gained him a place with Margate College Thirds.

"Eff it," said the girl, "my ankle's gone. You're the daft police inspector. I'm Stinting, Mr. Quarles will have told you. I got hit on the head and must have turned the ankle as I went down. What happened? Make it terse, man."

"Miss Sloper got it between the eyes. High-powered rifle as she went to the window drapes."

"Why they can't . . ." the girl stopped. "Get me up, I can limp back."

"You'll have to make a statement."

"I live in the village, but I'm not supposed to leave Sir Hugh's until eleven when the washing-up is finished. I got an hour off as per usual to go home for supper, as I only eat lunch in."

"Is he at home?"

"I think so. Cook is still there and old Jerry, the factotum."

"Get back and say nothing. Want me to take you?"

She wiggled a foot and exuded expensive perfume—a mistake in the overall cover, thought the Chief Inspector, though maybe these days domestic help did wear stuff at three quid the small bottle.

"You do not seem a very good bodyguard," she said demurely, "so I'd better hobble off myself. And, just as a friendly tip, cease that sliding tackle before you get your ears twisted off."

Harry watched her go, limping but trim buttocked, but the corner of his eye caught a dark shadow by the side of a Spanish elm. The lighting, though adequate when driving or walking, was patchy off the path. "Police here," he bleated, ego well deflated.

Chef Beedle stepped carefully on to the pathway, hands above his head. He had met police before, registered Harry, and not milksop English ones. "Put your hands down, man," he said quickly. "You're in Sir Alec's country now."

"That's what I'm afraid of," said the Chef, but lowered his hands. "I heard you talking and there is trouble. It is easy to pick on foreigners such as me and beat us."

"There is something wrong with your grammar . . ." began Harry.

"My grandma! I have none and if I have I'm not responsible," countered Beedle.

"Where have you been?"

"To Granchester, about Señor Abajo's rice. He is very fussy about it as the Spaniards are. You English do not understand rice."

"As you heard Miss Sloper was shot. There will be a policeman along tonight or tomorrow. Just go home and feed the Señor."

"He does not eat at night."

"Feed yourself, then." The Chef plainly thought it a good idea as he swiftly made off.

A police car whizzed past, and Harry saw the disapproving face of the local Super, a worthy man addicted to dog-breeding, boggling at him through the window. So the Chief Inspector trudged back to The Elms, making it a few seconds before the second police car and the ambulance. Honeybody, who had clearly put in a few minutes with the brandy bottle, was doing his butler act, displaying Miss Sloper as though she were the Master's family jewels.

". . . as a door-nail, gents," he was declaiming as Harry entered the now brilliantly lit room.

"A pretty how-do-ye-do, Chief Inspector," greeted the Super, who had a disconcerting habit of popping his dentures in and out when agitated. "Before your own eyes a pillar of the community, head of the Guides, president of the Women's Pleasant Hour, and God knows what else, is taken from us. What can we tell the *News of the World* let alone the *Sun*?"

His threnody was interrupted by a brusque technician with redbrick and efficiency stamped all over him.

"How was the light when the old girl bought it?"

"Dim," said Harry. "She was obviously a drinks-by-candlelight type and had only switched on that sidelight beside the bar."

"That means the murderer couldn't be sure who he was hitting," said the technician. "Considering the balance of light—between outside and in—he'd have seen a shape, like a black silhouette. Judging by the window and the angle, he was standing up. I'd say, cursorily, a three-o-three at maybe forty yards."

A man was chalking away at the parquet floor and flash bulbs winked. "Stone dead, fifteen minutes since," declaimed a little doctor. "I'll do the paper work tomorrow. Better get in touch with the relatives."

"Damned if I know whether she had any," sighed the Super. "That's your job, Chief Inspector. You saw the murder done!"

"It could have been me, or the Sergeant, according to your man," said Harry.

"A maniac? We've got thirty men in process of searching this Estate, two of them armed. Basically there are two main roads out. If there's a loonie with a rifle, we'll nab him within the hour."

"There was a car, I think," said Harry.

"I don't like that," said the Super. "The country fans out into a network of lanes and highways this side of Granchester. You can't check them all."

"I take it you didn't get the hit-and-run merchant who hit Miss Higgins?" counter-attacked Harry, conscious that he was being unfair.

The Super popped his teeth. "I think he might have been a local who made it back to his house. And, while you are on the subject, she discharged herself from hospital this afternoon. The quacks would have liked to detain her another couple of days, but she took off."

"That's odd," muttered Harry, "and in view of her association with Justin Title I don't like it much. I suppose she collected her car from the pub?"

"It's you and the Sergeant who live at the place!" The Super was getting mad and the scene might have become ugly had not the corpse been carried out at that moment and both men assumed a bowed head stance of reverent regret. As usual Honeybody hammed it up by clapping his old bowler hat to his plump chest.

A plain-clothes man came in. "Take a good day to search this place, that it will. Six filing cabinets filled with Girl Guides reports, closets stuffed with newspapers dating to 1900—her old aunt must have hoarded everything. Miss Sloper only lived in part of the house, so it seems. Her old girl is in her bedroom smelling of gin and heard nothing. I told her not to get up."

The Super pointedly did not offer Harry and Honeybody a lift back to the Marquis of Tenterton.

As they trudged back Harry reflected enjoyably that Miss Sloper was not his case and that it would be the Super who did not get to bed until three in the morning. Then a remembrance struck him. "It could have been you or me," he told Honeybody.

"I heard," said the Sergeant, "but there's been no criminal-lunatic escape this year. A skylarking teenager, p'raps."

"A professional killing job," said Harry, "and I'm damned if there are four men in the country capable of it. Three are inside and the fourth, Big Davie, is recovering—unfortunately for the world—from a car crash, but in no condition to do a killing."

"Why should anybody just want to kill somebody?" said Honeybody. "I don't like it, Harry, as I said before. That crafty-looking General would be a good shot, I guess."

"I don't think General Gould was good at anything," said Harry, "with the exception of being able to jaw the hindleg off a donkey in a public-school way. His manservant, an ex-sergeant, might be worth looking into because life with the General just might have driven him bonkers. I wish to God I could just go to old Palabras and ask him about the papers he's received."

"Why not, mate?"

"Because you bloody well don't do it thataway. It's Stealthy work, full of the Special Branch and M.I.5. Invisible ink, bugs, drops and all the childish paraphernalia which the Russians invented. But people get mysteriously run over in it, which reminds me of Miss Higgins. I'm off to London tomorrow: I'll tell Hawker that if I don't know more about the background I want out. I didn't much like the case in the first place and if I'm shot at I prefer to know why."

"Don't mind me," said Honeybody, "my dear wife being provided for."

"Sergeants are expendable, the General will back me there. While I'm bracing Hawker poke around. Try to get close to Palabras's old servitor."

"He's doyen of the public bar," said the Sergeant. "Percy McBean, a fit seventy-four from Sir Hugh's Scottish property. Haggis-bashing and burring by nature, but plays a wicked game of darts and likes whisky with beer chasers. He keeps an eye on Sir Hugh—knows his exact movements so that when the Master is out he can nick down for half an hour's darts and a couple of quick ones."

"Somebody approaching from behind," said Harry quietly, and they both swiftly wheeled. They were underneath one of the lamps, sitting ducks, but a fruity voice said: "We meet again, gentlemen."

It was the Vicar, Dr Tulkingham, wearing what looked like a green jump suit.

"I have to inspect my bird lime," he continued, "one gets

many pretty little warblers on balmy nights providing one uses Titcake, suitably crumbled."

"Miss Sloper has been murdered," said Harry, looking at the rubicund face rather closely. There was certainly no gun under the jump suit, but Dr. Tulkingham could have cached it.

"What will happen to my organ?" asked the Vicar aghast.

"Your what? I see, Miss Sloper was your organist."

"And her aunt before her. Miss Sloper was not adept and occasionally lapsed into the more unpleasant parts of Verdi during the voluntary, but, dear oh dear, how can I replace her? There *is* a girl of doubtful morals who can play the harmonium, but I think she is a Methodist! I must go and tell my wife. At this time of the year, when there is so much stuffing to be done, and fruits solicited for the Harvest Festival, this comes as a cruel blow."

Dr Tulkingham wheeled and trotted off on to one of the narrow side paths.

"He's the dodgy one," commented the Sergeant.

"I wouldn't mind having his income: I'd bet you he's evading tax. I must look him up in the clerical directory."

"He's a retired Army chaplain—church parades and all that. General Gould got him appointed because he covered up for him in 1944, said the old piker was praying for guidance when in reality he was down a funkhole cursing like hell. Or that's what they said in the public bar of the Marquis."

"Do they teach Army chaplains to shoot?" Harry was dubious.

" 'Course they do, in case the men turn on 'em."

Harry rose at five, had trouble getting out of the Marquis

of Tenterton, which does not boast a night porter. The landlord apparently believed in a complicated system of chains, padlocks and mortice locks with which the Chief Inspector wrestled in vain until he noticed a sign 'night bell'. Pressing this at last produced a sour-tempered Bosky Lane who let him out.

The first hour and a half was pleasant driving, but you cannot beat the English traffic and Harry edged through London in company with other people who had started equally early.

He found a telephone booth. Dianile Higgins was listed, but there was no reply. He remembered that her parents had something to do with U.N.O. and filled in time by having bacon and coffee at an early morning café before telephoning a friend at eight o'clock, being greeted by a sleepy voice.

"You are lucky," said the friend at last, "at least I think so. We have a Major and Mrs. Higgins on the cultural strength and they are currently in London boning up on a new assignment. They live in a ghastly service apartment in South Ken., named Twomey—I'll spell it—Mansions."

"What is the assignment?" asked Harry.

"Persuading Eskimoes to take up birth control so there won't be as many of them to interfere with the oil interests. There are problems, one understands, geared, as we say, to the intense cold, tee-hee." He was the kind of fellow who made a tee-heeing noise every so often, such as when somebody broke a limb.

"Do you know their daughter Dianile?"

"That is not a name but an epidemic. My breakfast is cooling fast. Give my regards to Major Higgins."

Hawker would not be available until ten, if then, the morning conferences occupying increasing time owing to discussion on the Irish Question: the top brass were busy swotting up on Gladstone and Parnell, with side dashes at

Michael Collins. Personally Harry advocated handing over what remained of the Commonwealth to Eire and allowing them to sort things out. So he parked his car with difficulty, pulling rank on a police constable in the process and feeling a cad about it. He caught a deserted bus going in the reverse direction from city commuters, and at nine entered the dingy but respectable confines of Twomey Mansions which sported a spotted and gloomy switchboard girl and some kind of clanking noise, possibly from the old hydraulic lift which eventually conveyed him to the third floor.

Retired majors who get themselves on the cultural racket are generally jolly coves, fond of their glass, but Major Higgins was not of this category. Behind glittering glasses he looked like a man whose service life had consisted of supervising the erection of quite excellent latrines. Harry mentioned his friend and his own rank and was ushered into the bleak breakfast-room—dining-room for the rest of the day—where Mrs. Higgins was at the end of the house phone complaining that the bacon she had recently consumed was rank. She was stout, blonde and efficient and possessed virtually no neck, but managed to swivel her head round enough to give him the benefit of her po face.

"I was sorry that your daughter Dianile had an accident, sir," said Harry.

"An accident!"

"The Food and Drug authorities shall be informed," snarled Madame Higgins into the house phone, "and I find your excuses inadequate. To be sure Wiltshire bacon is not what it was... pheasant for lunch, are you sure? Well, we'll see."

"What was this about Dianile? A free pheasant lunch and it had better be good, Horace. Assert yourself to the waiter. What about Dianile?"

"She sustained slight contusions and concussion from a hit-

and-run driver, Mrs. Higgins, at Waddington Parva. She discharged herself from Granchester Hospital yesterday, but it is necessary for us to take a brief statement..."

They did not seem particularly interested.

"Dianile has a flat and is on the telephone," said Mrs. Higgins.

"She is not answering."

"Waddington Parva," said Major Higgins. "That's where Hugh Palabras lives most of the time, Edith!"

"A friend of his?" enquired Harry.

"We know each other," said the Major with a certain coy modesty.

"And I suppose he knows Miss Higgins."

"I dare say he met her in her teens. A very fine man, Chief Inspector, who could have been the making of the country. He is always a little out of step, that is his trouble, and there are these trade unions which are the ruin of everything."

Harry, as usual wandering off the main scent, could not forbear to ask, "And I suppose you know dear old General Gould?"

There was no reply. Major Higgins adopted the expression he had probably used at the inspection of a particularly noisome sanitary installation. At length he said briefly that he personally was an 'enginah'.

"I suppose you would have no idea where Dianile might be?"

"She has her own life, which is as it should be," intoned Mrs. Higgins. "She is a courier, foreign countries have always fascinated her. When we were in Singapore she was always clambering around the Death Houses and absorbing local culture."

"Do you know a Justin Title?" asked the Chief Inspector.

"No," said the Major, almost in jocular fashion, "but I suppose he is one of Dianile's boy friends. She plays the field, but I dare say one day Mr. Right will come along and the wife and I will be grandparents."

"The coffee is atrocious," said Mrs Higgins, resuming her grasp on the house phone, "but perhaps you will have one. I shall, to cut the taste of that beastly bacon."

The Chief Inspector meekly agreed.

Major Higgins explained how the Eskimo diet of saturated fats not only prevented heart disease and caused them to live for inconvenient lengths of time, perpetually grumbling about the oil companies driving pipe lines and progress, but made them immune to the Pill.

"The United Nations is very worried about it," said Mrs. Higgins. "And of course the cold, which is intense, makes Old-Fashioned Methods impossible."

"Education," said the Major, as some atrocious coffee was borne in by a weary-looking Pakistani. "Appeal to their intelligence, not that natives have much in my experience, encourage them to see our educational films, and tax them very heavily. We of the Cultural Division find that the formula which works."

"Getting a bit short of dough, aren't you?" asked Harry as he spooned more sugar in to swamp the chemical flavour.

"As long as Oil is on our side we shan't want for the necessary." The Major pursed his lips and essayed a cunning wink. "And don't forget they control the rubber industry, so we'll be killing two birds for them, so to speak. In other places, such as India, the going is much tougher, but the Eskimoes seem fallow soil for the good word, or," he cackled, "the good oil."

Harry excused himself, setting down a half-filled coffee cup, and went to telephone Hawker who said he was busy until eleven. The Inspector hailed a gloomy taxi-driver (why were they always so bloody miserable at any time of day?) and gave an address in Whitechapel. The lair of Dr. Fu

Manchu seemed far away as he observed the smart aluminium-and-glass apartments. There were still some latter-day Fu Manchus around, though, and one was the gentleman named Charlie & Co., or simply 'The Big Co'.

Charlie had two ground-floor flats knocked into one and had picked it so there were four exits—five if you counted a loo window which opened out on to an alleyway. He opened the door himself and the smell of expensive aftershave streamed around Harry.

"My word, we're honoured," said Charlie & Co. with his leering, immaculately groomed smile. "Last week it was only a low Sergeant from the local station. Come in, sport, and take some coffee. I was just perking some up."

Charlie did not stint himself: the flat had everything that opened and shut, and there were good prints on the wall. Charlie had gone to Geelong Grammar and a little culture had rubbed off on him before he helped rob a bank at the age of nineteen.

Harry sat in the surprisingly comfortable Swedish chair and drank good coffee while he looked about. Then he said, "There was a man named Justin Title, an on-the-fringe merchant. He was going to get in touch with you about knocking over the Palabras house. The intermediary was Dianile Higgins."

"New to me, m'dear fellow, as the bride said," responded Charlie.

"I should tell you, Charlie, that this thing is big, with a lot of V.I.P.s with blood in their eyes. You should consider a bit of co-operation and then out of it. There is no percentage in digging your toes in, son."

"On the level?"

"I'm levelling, Charlie. Annoy us on this one, and we'll annoy you. Don't forget that old Sydney warrant: we could deport you for a starter."

"I could not get a month for that, even if the witnesses are still around, but deportation is something else. Frankly the dear old sunburned country might not be good for my health. Let me finish another cupper and think."

Finally the big gangster ran a manicured hand down one cheek and said, "There was an approach and a plan of the place—an easy safe behind a picture, one elderly servant and the Governor away politicking next Sunday. I quoted seven hundred nicker, two for me, the rest for the three boys I had in mind. It was papers they were after: blackmail, I thought, but, there, nothing to do with me. Truth to tell, I didn't too much like the sound of it. Title was a greasy rascal, not an honest thief, and there is a faint rumour that he once shopped a man in Ireland, though nobody knows the strong of it. I read he was dead and that was that."

"Not quite enough, Chas. Dianile Higgins went into the smoke after somebody came within a foot of killing her. I think you might know where she is."

"I wish I had never got into this bloody thing," whined Charlie, "you always get involved in other people's troubles through no fault of your own."

He was still playing for time, Harry knew. Charlie could assume practically any role from the outraged father or husband to the menacing collector of questionable gambling debts. "Get to tawses, Chas., as they say in the land of beer and cricketers."

"All right, she's here. I gave her a bedroom. Somebody tried to hit her, she can't think who. I've known Dianile three years. She's a good kid and you are bound to know her line of country. She took up with Title around the time I met her, he had an attraction for women, but then again it was part business with them. Oh, I've employed her and she is dead reliable. Upset, of course, but . . . well."

There was a small inter-house telephone and Charlie

pressed down a key. "A polite Chief Inspector drinking coffee, darl. You should join us."

"You just might be mixed up in politics, Chas., so back-pedal!" said Harry as the big Australian hung up.

"Christ!" said Charlie. "Not that! You know me, a Liberal supporter from way back, higher wool prices and sell the country to Japan by degrees. Politics I abominate except two whore-houses I own in Melbourne where the pay-off is high."

"This is one payment you should make," said Harry. "Maybe you'll get a life peerage."

Dianile Higgins came in. She had the matt skin that went with her colouring, and even disfigured by the bandage round her temples she was attractive, except for a certain evasive hardness.

"We kind of met the other night," said Harry.

"I'm grateful for everything you did," she said, drily, "including, one imagines, reading personal letters quite illegally taken from luggage."

"Now, my dear," said Charlie, "the Chief Inspector is known to be amiable and ingratiating, but he has a frightful old boss named Hawker who frightens thieves like me at twenty paces. Mr. James has told me that this is rather big. We don't want unnecessary trouble." A hard note came into Charlie's voice as he gritted out the last sentence.

"Justin's gone," said Dianile dully, "so it doesn't matter anyway. I don't quite know why I went to the Marquis of Tenterton."

"Money," said Charlie, without illusions.

"Oh, partly, one has to ruddy well live, but he was not the man to poison himself. When the real heat came on Justin simply disappeared, ran for it, and it had happened plenty of times from bits he told me. Once he holed up in

South Africa for six months, until it all blew over." She gave a faint, wry smile. "It always did blow over with Justin."

"What was the last job?"

"Sir Hugh Palabras had some papers . . . Justin reckoned there could be a minimum of five thou in it less the expenses of getting 'em. I didn't know the buyers."

Harry gave her a long look. She had a purplish bruise on one cheek-bone, and her left wrist and right knee were bandaged.

"Are you all right, Miss Higgins? I mean that we are not usually permitted to interview sick people unless they are dying which you demonstrably are not."

"Still life in the old girl, Inspector. I was lucky. I fell inwards and grabbed my own car. Another six inches out into the road, I guess, and no flowers by request."

"My Sergeant, who is an authority of some dubious sort, said you feigned unconsciousness."

"It's the best way," said Dianile, "in a tight corner you close your eyes and relax. *You* must know that. I didn't want questions. It was deliberate, my car being right tight against the parking kerb. If there was a murdering maniac about I might best pretend to be badly injured. For all the protection you fellows give once, he might have tried again."

"No clue?"

"I heard a car, that was all."

"Did you meet a Miss Sloper?"

"I heard she discovered me lying there. It might have saved him having another dash at me."

"She was shot between the eyes last night."

"Christ! Let me think!"

"Careful, petal!" drawled Charlie.

"I was here," said Dianile, "but I had met her the previous day. I'm an agent for one of those by-post cosmetic houses —it gets you in many places and the stuff is very good value.

I offered her a sub-agency—the Girl-Guide angle, harmless face creams and talc kind of things. I mentioned Justin. Cigarette me, Charlie."

The big man lit a cigarette and placed it between her lips.

"I'll be damned," said Miss Higgins slowly, "if I didn't believe she was laughing at me. Without pretences, I'm a crook..."

"We say operator, these days, dear," interposed Charlie. "The crooks are all in mutual funds."

Dianile smiled without much humour. "So my operator's mind thought there's more to Sloper than her Girl-Guide badge, much more, maybe. We had a brief interchange of how nice Justin had been, a cup of tea, and that was that. I used to see her eating at the pub, then that evening I spotted a fat police sergeant with you and thought maybe it was as well to clear out. I found no lead at all. Palabras is reputed to have a lot of old, valuable stuff around, but most of it is kept in a private wing with barred windows, and a steel-lined door with nice deep mortice locks. You'd need a torch unless you made it through the roof."

"How did Title know the documents in question were in the safe?"

"He had a tip-off. The last time I telephoned him he said one of the Palabras maids had sold him the info for thirty quid. He said she was a tough little bitch named Stinting. It made sense—the invisible-letter kind of ploy. No burglar in his senses would waste time opening a cheap, obsolete old can."

"Did you give the Palabras broad acres a good going-over?" enquired Harry, noting that she was looking rather tired.

"As part of the village. There was an old parson whose wife told me he was stuffing a bird, which turned out to be some kind of finch when I got in—he must have amused

Justin—the school headmaster who stammers and I think is rather Red, the publican who I can't place, a dark chef named Beedle who looks after an ancient Spaniard, the General and his rather unpleasant niece: a lot of unpleasant undertows. I shan't be sorry to escort a gaggle of young whores around Europe next month. At least they're predictable and come from the best schools. Oh, but Bruggles... I thought he was filming in Spain, playing a grandee with that great, handsome vacuous face of his."

"The theatrical knight who has the fourth house?"

"The same. Justin wrote that he hires staff through an agency when he spends the odd week here. A strange meld of people, that Estate. It was Sir Hugh's pa that collected them, offering peppercorn leases, because he liked odd people, and, by God, he got them. Except of course Miss Sloper, who told me that she inherited from an auntie."

"What about Bruggles? I'd heard he was in Spain."

"A rare old poofter, that darling of the stage," said Charlie.

"He's reputed to be an early riser because of indigestion and conscience. On the Sunday I got up at first light to case the Estate—just to get it in perspective as the landscaping makes it confusing. The other houses were dead, they all being rather late risers, so Justin had gathered. But as I came to Bruggles's house I saw what was apparently him scuttle through the open front door and shut it. As I know him I rang and knocked, but there was no reply. I thought he had returned unexpectedly with a 'friend'."

"At a guess, who did it?"

She had no hesitation. "Palabras, or somebody hired by him. Have you ever read his articles—he favours duelling and the stocks among other things."

"So do I," said Charlie. "There are a lot of people I would like to call out, and, strike me lucky, two days in the good old stocks is better than ten years in max. security or," he leered at Harry, "transportation to Tasmania."

"They used to chuck ordure over you."

"It kept order in Sir Hugh's good old eighteenth-cent. way, no doubt," chuckled Charlie.

"I'll have to leave you to the cross-talk: should you feel worse, Miss Higgins, get Chas. to introduce you with wisecracks to a doctor."

Superintendent Hawker had a new device for reducing his belly. Prone on his carpet he braced himself on what looked like the wheel of a minuscule bicycle. From this position at half past twelve he glared up at Harry before reluctantly requesting him to lend a hand. Hawker was getting feeble—all that lobster mayonnaise around Whitehall debilitating the nervous system as he grew more important to the Establishment—and he was breathing heavily as he subsided into his swivel chair and listened to Harry.

"The papers will give us hell," was his first reaction, but he pulled himself together as a tap at the inner door announced Mr. Quarles, as closely shaven and well soaped as the Chief Inspector remembered him.

"Well done," said Mr. Quarles, "you must be one of the first senior officers to see murder done, outside Indian mobs and nineteenth-century trades unionists. A rare sight." He chuckled with genuine mirth.

"For Christ's sake, Quarles, stop the production number. This Miss Sloper..." Superintendent Hawker stopped abruptly.

Mr. Quarles was flapping a hushing freckled hand. "To save beating around the bush, deceased was M.I.6. Retired, as much as you can retire from the job. Old naval family,

A FILE ON DEATH

Wren Officer from 1940 until Intelligence recruited her in 1946, good at languages and most competent. A paymaster was wanted and she was given a crash course in accountancy. It is difficult work requiring utmost discretion and occasionally ingenuity of high order. She ostensibly ran a typing agency at Fulham. She was with the Service for eighteen years, retiring when an aunt died leaving her the residue of a lease on the Palabras Estate."

Mr. Quarles cleared his throat. "It was fortuitous but fortunate to have somebody acquainted with surveillance living close to Palabras. He is a dangerous man: several Prime Ministers have realised his potential. Miss Sloper had qualified for a pension of seventeen pounds per week; she was given a further five plus audited expenses for submitting a weekly report upon Sir Hugh." He inspected an expensively covered crossed leg.

"Look here," said Hawker, "I'm not a baby. There is evidence—lousy evidence—" he glared at Harry—"that Sloper was in touch with Justin Title and that these fornicating papers plus several thousand quid were mentioned."

"One of the reasons that no obstacle or inducement not to do so was placed in the way of Miss Sloper upon retirement," said Quarles, "was that the evaluation of her security risk showed some alarming implications. You see, as in Roman times when ciphers were kept on knotted string, the security agent is loyal to the *de facto* government. If that changes so does his loyalty. There really is no other way to work it. Miss Sloper was becoming an anarchist: she increasingly believed in small, self-contained country communities. She kept Cobbett's *Rural Rides* in her desk drawer and in her holidays retraced his steps in her motor car."

"Then it seems strange that you kept her on," said Harry.

"Oh, she had no time for Palabras's eighteenth-century fascism, or for his big-business connections. She knew about the papers, but *we had not commissioned her to spend money on their retrieval.*"

"Had she money?" barked Hawker.

"The family died out and after death duties she was worth probably eighty-five thousand pounds, plus a valuable lease and valuable furniture. You will ask me what kind of woman she was. The answer is that she was pretty deep," Quarles paused for half a second, "and of course the Department was in error. Subtlety we like, deepness not. She liked small children and animals, an un-British and possibly dangerous trait, but her breeding and background were impeccable—went back beyond Nelson. What her motives were we do not know, but she exceeded her instructions. Perhaps she had gone off her head, it is a departmental risk."

"Love affairs?" asked Hawker.

"She was a determined spinster. Men liked to ask her out to dinner, but that was all. She was well read and not unwitty."

"Your Miss Stinting tipped off Title where the papers are kept," said Harry.

"Under instruction," said Quarles. "She picked him up, being a very adept operator and excellent on dialogue. We frankly hoped that Title would set up the job and that then we could apprehend the thieves. Q.E.D."

"How did Title get his own information?" persisted Harry.

"My dear fellow, the existence of them is now known in every ruddy Embassy in Europe. Thank God we got rid of all those Russians, otherwise we'd have been in a state of siege. As it is, somebody got wind of her activities and shot poor Miss Sloper. We have arranged for the Lord Lieutenant to attend the obsequies, a final last tribute."

"There is a Chef Beedle..."

"When cooks go off the rails they are nasty, most of them

suffering from acute indigestion, mild dipsomania and hallucinations. Beedle is classed as a revolutionary, but rather too hot in his culinary politics, as it were, for his fellow Afros to take."

"He said something out of turn. I was alone and he excused himself by saying he had heard me talking and that something was up. He must have been around the house."

"I can't see it as Beedle," said Quarles. "Directing a rabble is more his line—and fishing in troubled waters, which I suggest he might have been doing. Keep him under scrutiny, because if he knows anything he would attempt blackmail or intimidation. And now . . ." Quarles looked at Harry and his eyes were not nice, "you must surely apply for a warrant to search the Palabras house, every damned inch of it. Mr. Hawker will send down his best search squad, and a man of mine, for identification purposes, will be among them. Tomorrow morning at noon!"

"I do not see how I can connect up a case" said Harry.

Quarles wrinkled his upper lip. "Miss Stinting will depose that she saw Palabras at the scene of the crime. She can retract later if it should become necessary. You can assuredly get a warrant on her evidence."

"I do not like it."

"You are acting under orders for the good of the state," said Quarles, calmly and coldly. "We are constantly harassed by wicked men without scruples and sometimes we have to do strange things." He collected his soft black hat. "I expect a report by six p.m. tomorrow. 'Day to you both."

Even before the door closed Hawker was wrenching the top off his antacid powder, while Harry thoughtfully filled him a glass of water.

"It's either this or getting old at Bournemouth," said the Super when he felt a little easier in the stomach.

"Anybody could have shot Miss Sloper," said Harry, "but

the point is that she was wearing a severely tailored outfit and she was tall for a woman, while I am short for a policeman. An expert said it would have been impossible to distinguish exact detail."

"Experts!" pished Hawker. Wise in the old man's ways, Harry detected a kind of shiftiness.

"I mean that it could have been me, making a lovely case for a search warrant."

"Somebody bashed this Stinting woman," countered Hawker.

"So she said. I did not examine the bitch myself and under the circumstances I could not pull her in."

"I do not like the role of this woman Higgins," said Hawker, changing the subject.

"The entire truth is not in her, of course," said the Chief Inspector, "and there were questions I could have asked but did not. I did not want to frighten her or Charlie, who has a good brain. There were discrepancies in her statement, perhaps better described as omissions. I want her under maximum surveillance and to be pulled in for questioning if she tries to leave the country. She'd know all the back doors so tell 'em not to give her too much leeway."

"There are too many private yachts," Hawker expressed a perennial police grumble. "Well, you might as well come along and lunch with me." He was affability itself, and over coffee and brandy talked about his water colours.

Chapter Four

SERGEANT HONEYBODY, WHO hated the country had nevertheless spent a peaceful and contemplative day, not unmixed with cunning. He had consulted the Coroner's officer and made a statement concerning Miss Sloper's death, made the discovery that a bottle of government-provided brandy was available in the morgue for people who became overwrought, which Honeybody promptly became in company with the Coroner's officer, and by guileful methods fallen in with General Gould's man, ex-Staff-Sergeant Bottomley, a square man with the remnants of red hair. It was his day off, and he preferred the more modest attractions of the Goat, a beer, cider and perry house at the end of the village, so he and Honeybody quaffed in slippered ease. He confided that the local prolies were yokels and no company for a man who had travelled the world. In turn the Sergeant said that in his provincial travels it was a treat to meet a man who knew anything further than the local bus stop.

In spite of his colouring, Bottomley had been known to his subordinates as 'The Black Bastard', a fact which Honeybody had no difficulty in accepting. He had also killed quantities of krauts, wops, wogs and two Americans by mistake, which the Sergeant doubted, judging that Mr. Bottomley was shrewd enough never to have ventured into an actual area of combat except through faulty map-reading.

"And a good Guv'nor to work for once the heat of the

day, as the poet says, is o'er,'" pontificated Honeybody. "A foxhunting man and a gent."

"I heard him say that the 'ounds are worth thirteen 'undred a year to him," said Bottomley, whose aspirates tended to suffer in drink, "as well as commissions from the horse-copers, saddlers, tailors, etcetera, who he recommends the young blokes to. 'E provides the catering for the 'unt ball at seven guineas the ticket, and if it costs him a quid, jobbed out to the Granchester caterers, I'm a Dutchman."

"The gentry have to keep up appearances," said Honeybody, "and whatever your rank, the bit of pension they give you doesn't keep your soul-case on. It stands to reason that the General has expenses, and a niece, too, to support, a Mrs. somebody."

"Peremely-Fox," said Bottomley and graphically described what he thought the lady needed. "But she has cash of her own—reefed the lot off her old man before he scarpered to sunny Spain: best day's work he ever done if you ask me. The old bitch came to live with the Guv'nor on a paying basis—trust him—because she thought she could get into the talking shop on his influence, but the local association prefers old Kiddle, who made his money out of fish shops and is pretty liberal with it when he thinks it'll do him good. Gladys—Mrs. Peremely-Fox—keeps every penny locked up in her drawers and if anybody holds their hand out she gives them good advice, she's got plenty of that!"

"Sounds like the General!"

"She should have been the General—at least she's got guts and can shoot."

"Shoot, eh?"

"Her hobby, target shooting. She's as good as I've seen and I was an instructor once."

"I suppose she got on with Miss Sloper, Girl Guides and all that?"

"Mrs. Peremely-Fox thinks that the Girl Guides are run by the Russkis," said Bottomley, "and she thought that old Sloper was a Commo because she saw her buying a tube of Swedish caviar paste at the supermarket. She often said Sloper was Up to No Good. Did I ever tell you about that Russian girl I met in Vienna in the good old days when we had a slice of it?"

Sergeant Honeybody, who had scabrous stories of his own, chiefly centred around the English Midlands, resigned himself.

Thus it was that eventually Chief Inspector James arrived at the Marquis of Tenterton very shortly after Sergeant Honeybody, who was greasy from pea soup with pigs' trotters and a nice piece of black pudding to follow.

Harry was tired after the drive and sat on the corner of his bed in dour silence while Honeybody reported. The Sergeant's weight made the frail bedroom chair creak and groan.

"I've come to one conclusion, not a popular one," he said at last. "If we find who killed Title, and I'm convinced he was killed now, we've got the person who shot Sloper and probably tried to put Dianile Higgins in hospital if not the morgue."

"The maid who did his room is an old grandma who reads and writes with difficulty," said Honeybody. "Loves her drop of stout, has buried her old man and six children and does not spare the details, works so she can have a bob or two on the ponies and thoroughly enjoys life. You can't see her murdering anybody. She even goes to church, but they say that the Vicar tips her three bottles of port every Good Friday. He's dead scared that the Church

Commissioners will abolish the living, so he bribes a few of the prolies to attend the services. They say that when the Archdeacon is making a call he can raise fifty farm labourers at half a bottle of Scotch per man, all looking reverent."

"He kept his door locked?"

"Old Lane is hot on that. You can't get past the reception desk without him whining at you about leaving the key. And if he's not there it's the porter. It must have been somebody sliding in while he was in the bathroom."

"And where does that leave us?" Harry was fed up.

"With Bosky Lane." The chair creaked as Honeybody scratched his stomach.

"What?"

"The biopsy report said that various kinds of barbiturates were used, a kind of brew of the bloody things. Now people often leave things in pubs, p'raps two or three tablets in a bottle, particularly if they feel groggy in the morning. Lane has a rule that everything left in the rooms is delivered to him. There is a cupboard in the poky little office of his. When I say everything, that includes old newspapers, which he puts in a sack to be sold as waste paper. It's his thing, his mania. He unknots and keeps bits of strings and fusses over the electric lights being on."

"But why the hell should he do it? I mean it's an attractive idea because he'd have the key in his possession when Title was out. But Title booked in here, he'd hardly have done that if Lane was gunning for him."

"I couldn't find anybody who saw Lane when Miss Sloper was killed," said Honeybody.

"Your informant being the barmaid, and how would she stand up in the box?"

"A little chivalry, please, Chief Inspector," reproached Honeybody, "she being a fine figure of a woman and her word as good as any woman's, which don't say much. But

Lane wasn't there at the relevant time, as far as Doris can ascertain with discreet enquiries. The staff don't like Lane very much, because he knows all the angles and is apparently dead honest himself. He doesn't even fiddle on bottle sales, which is what they normally all do."

Harry made an entry in his notebook as he was supposed to do. He winced at the thought of the expense of toothcombing through Bosky Lane's life in search of a link with Justin Title that might have resulted in murder, hundreds of man-hours expended and an official frown in the direction of the Chief Inspector who recommended it. There was a little ray of brightness: as a publican Lane's career would have been documented, at any rate as far as places and times were concerned. The actual references would be fairly worthless as most references are.

"I wonder if they met in Ireland?"

"There's an age-group difference that would be difficult to bridge. Lane is pushing sixty, twenty years more than Title's age, and hasn't been to Ireland for years, so the staff say. He takes a fortnight off each year salmon-fishing. Palabras lets him use the lodge in Scotland which is one of his possessions."

"How thick are Palabras and Lane?"

"A faithful-steward relationship. Bosky butters up Sir Hugh nicely, but not too nice if you understand my meaning. A kind of cosy squire-and-butler relationship. There is apparently some genuine liking between them, and of course Lane gets well paid with a fair amount of fringe benefits."

"I have to apply for a warrant to search the Palabras house."

Honeybody whistled, then said, "I wouldn't want to be in that one, Harry, or to see you in it. When it's question time in the Commons and one of Palabras's cronies puts one, they'll drop you like a hot coal. 'The officer in question exceeded his instructions and has been put on traffic duty on Wigan Pier.' There was that case of old Jones—three weeks off retiring and then asked for his resignation on half-pension."

"That's not quite the same: he lost his head."

"Only after Somebody hinted pretty strongly that it was his duty to break up that south London gang at all costs, so Jonesy went round planting bugs—'an affront to our democratic conscience' said a lady M.P. Jones was a broken man in all senses of the word! Have you got written orders?"

"No."

"Ask for 'em!"

"I'd be on Wigan Pier a damn sight quicker. There's nothing I can do."

"Just ask Palabras straight out where he's got the papers. That'll do for a start."

"You must be joking!"

"There are two things about Palabras. First, he's a gent, Gawd help us: second, he's rather too honest for his own good. A lot of the prolies are for Palabras because they sense these qualities. He's not mealy-mouthed, however much in the clouds his head may be. Let's nick over and put it to him. I heard Arthur Johnston do something similar over the Streatham Monster case. He was Super then, and he just went up to this fellow, Case by name, and said 'What about making a clean breast of it, old man' and, stap me, the fellow did just that. They get this violent craving to unburden themselves."

Harry looked at his watch. Five fifteen, a good time to catch people at home; and Honeybody's hunches were quite often right.

"You had better walk over with me," he sighed, "in case I need a witness."

It was a nice afternoon and Harry did not hurry because

he desired to postpone an unpleasing chore. There were still policemen about the Estate, peering and prodding into the shrubbery, by which the Chief Inspector surmised that they had not found what the dimmer newspapers called 'the fatal weapon'.

"Did they get anything from the bullet?" he asked Honeybody.

"The morgue keeper told me it had hit bone and disintegrated, but from the obvious velocity it might be one of those fancy U.S. target rifles. To use them requires a certain amount of expertise."

"Not Americans, that's all I want!" groaned Harry.

"The local Sergeant said there was a suspicious American woman living in a tent, but she turned out to be a man who writes country-style music and is terrified of guns."

The old, faithful servitor answered the door. At his second visit to the house Harry had more opportunity of admiring its relaxed comfort and a harmony bred of money but not stinking of it.

This time Sir Hugh was in his library, a large room with French windows which overlooked a small plantation. This was obviously offbeat for the Vicar and Harry said so, because sundry late afternoon twitterings could be heard.

"You can't stop the Vicar stuffing birds," said Sir Hugh. "There's no law against it unless the species is protected, and it's not poaching. And I could not add to the enormity of my ogrish reputation by persecuting the Cloth. As long as he does not catch my particular favourites I shall leave him alone."

"I suppose the locals pestered you about Miss Sloper's death, Sir Hugh?"

"Hardly that . . . oh, I was seated here at the relevant time doing an article for the *New Politician*. Obviously I could have slipped out and shot the woman. My late father collected guns and we have a gun-room. I gave the local police the key. I suppose somebody, probably the handyman, cleans them occasionally. My personal armoury consists of two shotguns which I keep at my Scottish place, but m'father was a fanatic. After visiting his tailor he inevitably visited his bespoke gunsmith. In point of fact the dear fellow was a horrible, rotten shot."

"I suppose you are a good one?"

"I won a competition in the O.T.C. and did the usual Army course in 'thirty-nine, but I do not recollect handling a rifle since nineteen forty-four." Sir Hugh smiled genially.

"I don't imagine you had much reason to kill her," said Harry.

"I'd like the whole four of my tenants out of the way, but they all have leases, granted by my father in weak-minded moments, which have at least from twenty to thirty years to run, and their heirs would merely take over. Miss Sloper's heir is a lecturer at the London School of Economics, for God's sake, with four particularly horrible, Communist-orientated children, three with acne, and a wife who writes scripts for the Third Programme. It is enough to drive a man to drink."

Honeybody immediately brightened, but Palabras went no further. Instead he said, "I did not tell the locals, considering it might be out of their orbit, but I was aware that Miss Sloper had spent some years in Military Intelligence."

"She told you?"

"My dear sir, it isn't a thing you discuss like the price of corn. I had, in 1946, considerable connections in Eastern Europe, more or less by accident of birth. The Government pocketed its pride and gave me an advisory position. I knew that Sloper was an executive on the financial side. I met her when there was a problem of getting some money through to Warsaw—it was a mad kind of business with fake merchant banks and trading companies. We never referred to the matter when she came here."

"I'm afraid, Sir Hugh, that I shall have to apply for a search warrant. Better for you to co-operate and get thoroughly cleared."

"A typical Quarles stupid gambit," sighed Sir Hugh. "I taught him anything he may know about politics. It amused me to do so. He was a horrible example of a scholarship boy and an early prototype of Red-Brick culture. His accent was deplorable and he wore spectacles. One is informed that he now speaks clipped Whitehall, collects eighteenth-century snuff boxes, patronises young poets and wears contact lenses. You know what this is all about?"

"I know about some documents."

Sir Hugh had the disconcerting habit of never quite losing a smile and Harry sensed that he was a man whose very presence could be annoying. "The day you saw me, Chief Inspector, I said I had an appointment. I kept it and delivered the documents to a very trusty friend who placed them in a bank vault the following day."

"So you intend to publish them or cause them to be published?"

"That is not policeman's pigeon, neither could I acknowledge the contemplation of an offence against the Official Secrets Act."

"Yet you eventually will be charged, I would think."

"Once the first instalment hits the street and the syndication rights have been arranged—oh, it'll be bigger than the Macnamara Papers—the Establishment will be chary of proceeding. I ate my dinners and was admitted to the Bar as a youngster, thought it might be useful, so I should defend myself and I have a certain vituperative talent. There are a few whited sepulchres I should like to examine in a court of law." A tic twitched over Palabras' right eye as he mentioned a few names.

"But what good will it all do?" said Harry. "Weaken the pound, put Joe Bloggs, the honest garage mechanic, on social security, ruin a few men who will chuckle as they prepare to enjoy well-endowed retirement."

"Mr. Bloggs may be due for something worse than social security if certain persons remain whose moral corruption equals their inefficiency. I am a believer in completely open diplomacy and fearless enquiry into the cause of mistakes. From nineteen forty-four on I asked 'why?', 'where did that money go?' and they shut me up by telling me it must wait until Victory. Then I spoke again, to be told about spilt milk, not looking back, being constructive and the golden horizon ahead if the mines would only produce more coal. Now I have certain of the bastards by the short hairs."

"Thirsty work, sir," said Honeybody.

"I forgot policemen liked beer," Sir Hugh grinned. "Would you like something?"

"Not for me," said Harry.

"It's been a long hard day, and overtime is not allowable, so a pint might oil my uvula in preparation for the evening's work," replied his minion.

Sir Hugh pushed a button and a section of bookcase swung out to reveal a neat refrigerated space. "Come to think of it a good pint, well chilled, might go nicely in today's heat. I will join you, Sergeant."

Harry thought that he was being gently needled as Sir Hugh produced two refrigerated silver tankards and emptied out two pint bottles. "I fear our old friend Quarles thinks only dry sherry is genteel," smiled the baronet and the Chief Inspector felt a little foolish. "Never be forced into doing something you think is wrong," had said his housemaster and Harry realised uneasily that this was about the first time in his life that he had actually obeyed the dictum.

"Well, Chief Inspector," said Sir Hugh as he toasted a radiant-visaged Sergeant Honeybody, "I hope you believe me."

"As far as the papers go, yes," said Harry, smile for smile. "I suppose you kept them in that old safe in your workroom."

"One always attributes the art of subtlety to oneself," said Sir Hugh. "It seemed a good idea because the obvious place was my private suite which would take a hell of a lot of getting into. One thought of treachery, modern laser technology, etcetera, and decided to leave the papers in the safe. But it's one of those Chinese box puzzles—do you try the obvious or not? Childish in a way, because I should have known the best place is a bank vault, which can only be opened after long legal procedure! Good beer this, about the only brew left that the chemists haven't ruined! I'm glad you believe me: no point really in my lying even if it were a habit of mine."

"I suppose those documents are genuine?" said Harry.

Sir Hugh looked disconcerted. "Genuine? I recognised prose styles under all that jargon, and the signatures. Good God!" But he was uncomfortable and Harry gave him a few minutes to think before Palabras said. "I see, you are hoping I shall nip into the car at nine tomorrow and hare up to the bank. Good try, me lad, but the cock won't fight."

Harry changed the subject. "About your fourth tenant . . ."

"The immortal Bruggles! The most brainless actor, one believes, that trod a board, to coin a phrase. My father thought he was a genius—a profile when young which reminded old ladies of John Barrymore, the most beautiful voice since Henry Ainley and . . . the brains of a cockroach and I don't mean Archie. But an infinite talent for survival. He wisely mostly sticks to Shakespeare, which is mainly music for the average theatre-goer, a voice declaiming and a lot of good sets. Then, of course, he gets some juicy film parts still. Character stuff which he does competently enough: he has three expressions, sly, outraged and noble resignation, which he learned at the R.A.D.A. in the twenties. Directors know his capabilities, the old faggot, and middle-aged women love him. Harmless," Sir Hugh gave the tip of his nose a tweak, "at least I *think* so, though once upon a time when I proposed some change in his lease, wanting to cut down some trees and replace 'em, the old tabby flew to solicitors and showed his claws right and proper. Since then I've had reservations, but he's away filming in Spain and has been for three months, *Torquemada meets Count Dracula,* one imagines the title to be."

"There is some suggestion that he might be in his house."

You did not have to dot your i's with Sir Hugh.

"He gets staff on a contract basis through an agency," he said swiftly. "Nobody there permanently. A firm in Granchester sends a van with power equipment over each Monday to do the garden—he has it with a couple of lawns, the trees and some shrubs." He gave a short laugh. "The house is bedizened with flowers like an old whore when he's at home, but they are presents from admirers. Nasty people say that Bruggles might be his own admirers. I suppose he could have sneaked back with a boyfriend or alone even. He's got electrical heating so if he wanted a fire at night there would be no smoke. It gets a little chilly at nights and Bruggles loves his comfort. Come to think of it, Bruggles is hardly the chap to batch, but maybe the boyfriend has a light touch with the pastry and can make beds and valet." Sir Hugh chuckled.

"It's an odd situation," said Harry, "if the good knight is holed up in his house with an adequate supply of food in the freezer, I'm darned if I know what we can do except beat vainly at the door."

Sir Hugh reached for the telephone and dialled. "No

A FILE ON DEATH

reply," he said at length, "but," he hesitated, "m'father had a thing about fire. As a boy it seemed to me we were surrounded by extinguishers, patent escape ladders and rows with hotels because Father insisted on living on the ground floor which was always noisy. One of the clauses in the leases is that we—the family—have a key to the front doors of the other four houses, in case fire breaks out when the tenants are away." Sir Hugh opened the door cupboard in the side of his desk and rummaged around, producing a key ring with four imposing-looking keys upon it. "Good locks," he commented, "and changed every two years—another of m'dad's fads. He used to read Edgar Wallace and was convinced you could take impressions with a bar of soap. I spent hours as a kid trying, but merely bunged the holes up."

"They use a thing called a slap-hammer which removes the tumbler in four seconds flat," said Harry absently. "No mucking about in this day and age. I suppose you could make a landlord's visit, smelling smoke or something. Nothing illegal in it if we didn't pinch Bruggles' *crème de menthe*, which one is told he drinks with lemonade."

Sir Hugh shuddered and squinted at the key ring. "Here it is, marked number three. Suppose we get it over with. It's a matter of ten minutes' walk, over behind the beeches, p'raps the best designed of the four houses."

Sir Hugh opened the French windows and they walked along trim paths between bowling-green grass. "I like well-tailored grass," he said, "this bit having taken two hundred years of manicuring. When nobody heeds the name Palabras it will still be here—or so I hope. I'm leaving the Estate to the National Trust, suitably endowed, though future socialist governments may decide to turn it into an automatised workhouse for young unemployed people. There it is, the residence of Bruggles, the mecca of every faggot of the western world."

Not more than forty years old, thought Harry, unlike the

other three which were more likely four times that. It had a portico flanked by two windows masked with venetian blinds. Sir Hugh inserted the key and twisted and the door swung back. Within was richness, but a theatrical richness as though old but valuable sets from lush Edwardian plays had been used to furbish it. Even the heavy red carpet was 1928 cinema-ware.

"Coo!" said Honeybody. "Like Madam Mavis's whorehouse that used to be in the Edgware Road when I was starting."

"Starting what?" Sir Hugh was amused.

"A life spent improving public morals," said Honeybody, eyeing the many gilt photographs—'To darling Bruggles'—inset along the eggshell-blue walls.

"The man has atrocious taste," said Palabras, "but there don't seem to be anyone home."

"There's a smell of fresh cigar smoke," Honeybody had a beagle nose. "Expensive grade, none of the old Dutch cabbage."

"Bruggles doesn't smoke, frightened of his voice production."

"Excuse me," Harry raised his voice. "Police here. Police here!" A door opened along the hallway and the alarmed face of the elderly actor, by instinct and training registering emotion a little larger than life, peered out. "Oh, Hugh!" He relaxed.

"Thought I sniffed smoke," Palabras was genially false.

"Oh, dear," said Bruggles, grimacing, "it would be my friend's cigars. Special Cuban ones, so hard to get, so expensive and so nasty."

"Your friend or the cigars?"

"Naughty old baronight," camped Bruggles, ogling the Chief Inspector with some interest. "Well, I suppose you won't want to stay as everything is under control."

"Now I'm here, there are a few matters you might help us on." Harry gave an admonitory snap to the rubber band around his notebook, much as some ladies produce a disapproving sound from their suspender belts.

"Help?" Bruggles managed to sound like a Wilde duchess at bay.

"Miss Sloper was shot last night."

The rest of Bruggles, pyjama trousers and smoking jacket included, sidled through the door into the hallway. He had no intention of inviting them in. "You mean with a bullet?"

"This is drama, not low comedy," said Harry grimly.

"The old bitch did get on the sauce occasionally," declared Bruggles. "My dear, I've seen her reeling her way home, no doubt after a Girl-Guide meeting. She was a shifty old bitch, no good being sentimental about it. Always watching people out of the corner of her eye and asking little, digging questions."

"When did you get back? Everyone thought you were filming in Spain."

"For once they were ahead of schedule. The director is an accountant!" Bruggles snorted. "And well, there was a *contretemps*." He had the actor's trick of allowing a word to float in the air like a small neat parcel while he eyed it. "A *contretemps*," he repeated with approval. "It is entirely private, but it has made it necessary, or rather desirable, for me to, ah, lie low for a few weeks. Men of the world, eh?"

He was a rather nasty old creature, realised Harry.

"I suppose you have an alibi for last night?" asked Harry.

"Such a nuisance having the place shrouded, masked as it were, so no light shines without. But we prepared a nook, in what is the butler's pantry, with hot plates and heating plus books and we certainly did not go out."

"Could I see the we in the alibi?"

"Afraid not, my dear. My guest is the *contretemps*, 'nuff

said. All sorts of complications and ravings. Very jealous, the Spanish in general. It comes of their unfortunate cuisine, all those frightful little red chillis and eggs with garlic. Perhaps I should phone my lawyer. I mean you have no warrant, and it is idle to suppose I would shoot drunken old guidesses, or goddesses unless it is one of those dreadful old Greek things that I was never much good in."

"If you had a guess, who would kill Miss Sloper?"

Bruggles put the knife in. "Sir Hugh, I yield you the privilege! An old trooper learns to use his eyes: you have to if you want to eat. And my genial old landlord did not like Miss Sloper at all."

"You *are* a prize old bitch," said Palabras, with nothing but admiration discernible in his voice.

His comment was greeted by the radiant smile which Harry remembered had so impressed him when Bruggles played Jesus Christ in a film directed by somebody he had now forgotten. Coincidentally with the radiance Bruggles popped through the door and there was the sound of a moved bolt.

"You have got to hand it to him," said Palabras, "as a veritable bag of bitchery right through the years. God knows how many beginners the perennial old rotter has upstaged or hounded out of the profession. He doesn't even like dogs or cats."

The fresh air was pleasant.

"I suppose Bruggles would be open to blackmail," mused Harry.

"Not now, really," said Palabras. "He was the son of a Lambeth publican who got things the easy way. He wouldn't kill a fly except verbally. If I got an anonymous letter I'd suspect Bruggles, but if somebody fired a shot at me I'd acquit the fellow even if he had a gun in his hand."

Harry stared up at the flying clouds. "And did you hate

Sloper? I mean, he is right about actors being pretty shrewd observers."

Palabras's face said nothing. "I'm a bit too old in the tooth to hate." He sounded tired. "Suppose we go back and have a drink, wash the taste of darling Bruggles off the palate."

"A policeman's work is never done," said Harry, "but perhaps another day when there is a respite."

In spite of almost open mutiny on Honeybody's part they went their separate ways.

"I doubt the bit about Sir Hugh being beyond hatred," the Chief Inspector presently said to his sulky underling.

"Impetuosity was his downfall," grunted the Sergeant. "I wouldn't trust him to plan more than a short time ahead, though o' course, a man like that has the dough to hire planners. Look, here comes our Fleet Street friend."

"Isn't it terrible?" panted Miss Drinkwater, clutching a large bundle. "I've been over to Señor Abajo. That ass Chef Beedle told him, though one must say the old gent took it calmly. I suppose at that age a bullet means little. He's lending some books to Palabras, who reads Spanish well."

"I suppose you have an alibi?"

"Pure as snow, but poor old Sloper buying it like that!" A flash of Fleet Street shrewdness showed through her grief. "Though she would pry, you know. A pathological pryer was she, embarrassing at times. I suppose the poor lady stuck her nose into something that was dangerous."

"Could be," said Harry non-committally, "some people die like that. I suppose old Abajo is incapable of mayhem? He was alone at the time."

"I imagine the *señor* has a different view on killing people from us," said Miss Drinkwater, "but the poor old chap is a cabbage. Up to the time that Chef Beedle appeared on the scene six months ago he was entirely at the mercy of constantly changing nurse-housekeepers. They always left, the countryside not being to their taste, and we ladies plus the district nurse had to cope. He won't go into an institution—says they kill you there or else painfully prolong your life—but Beedle copes marvellously."

"Any idea who killed Sloper?"

"Suppose it was Lane who runs the pub? She mostly ate there and was always needling old Bosky as though she had something on him, which seems impossible. You can't get any sly grog at the Marquis or buy a hot radio. Still, he's Irish..."

"There is an Irish thread through this beastly tapestry," groaned Harry. "Justin Title being a slippery leprechaun if there ever was one his size. I suppose Miss Sloper was not Irish?"

"Welsh," said Miss Drinkwater, "from Swansea way."

Harry thanked her and walked in silence beside Honeybody to the Marquis of Tenterton. Quick at ascertaining a mood, the Sergeant opined that he would spend the evening at Granchester, providing a taxi was authorised. The Chief Inspector readily agreed. "Sloper ate out a lot, see if you can get any background. There is something niggling at the back of my mind: but somebody must have known quite a bit about Justin Title and Miss Sloper, which means enquiries by somebody skilled at it!"

The local Superintendent had left a message for Harry to call on him. In spite of his ill-fitting dentures and a tendency to warts, he was a man without vices, except a liking for weak tea, and had a prodigious capacity for work. It was rare, he assured Harry, for him to quit his cluttered little desk before the church clock registered midnight. The tea was served in rather pleasant, large cups, but the thin cucumber sandwiches were on plates which invited you to visit an obscure seaside resort. All in all, thought Harry, looking at the mottled redness of the Super's nose, it seemed to matter little whether you ruined your digestive juices one way or the other.

"Not your pigeon," said the Super, "but we have not found that ruddy gun! I'm pretty sure it was not taken out by car—we did a smartish job there—but we couldn't find it. Sir Hugh was co-operative: there's a lot of valuable hardware in the gun-room, but nothing recently fired or indeed anything suitable for the operation. Nothing in the line at Señor Abajo's, and the General possesses only two shotguns. Miss Sloper didn't possess any kind of weapon except bows and arrows used for archery."

"Bruggles?" asked Harry.

"He's away in Spain."

"Not so." Harry explained.

"He wouldn't kill a fly," said the Super. "They say he's scared of the *papier-mâché* swords they use in the bloodier bits of Shakespeare. But who can he be shacked up with?"

"As long as he doesn't stir out of the house," said Harry, "there is nothing we can do about it. It's a bizarre situation, but a man is entitled to have a guest in his house without molestation. In any case one can hardly imagine an assassin coming to Waddington Parva in such circumstances."

"That damned gun," said the Super and swore picturesquely. "However, I have something for you. The analysis of Justin Title's brandy, or what remained of it, showed traces of seven proprietary sleeping pills, including one rare one of French origin. It is rarely prescribed anywhere and is only obtainable in Europe on prescription. The trade name is Cyclalinometo. A Frenchwoman stayed in the pub last August and left six in a pill box. The chambermaid picked them up, and the name sunk in. She is a keen cyclist herself and thought the name 'ever so queer'. A girl of eighteen, engaged to one of my young constables. She only lasted two months at the Marquis: no fault of hers, just didn't like the life in a pub. She is dead sure, though I will say that once she gets an idea into her head it never comes out." He sighed and poured out more tea.

Harry knew that type of witness. In their efforts to be fair the police rather avoided them, besides which a smart counsel had not much difficulty in exposing the immensity of their prejudice to the jury.

"She gave it to Bosky Lane," said the Super, "and he put it into a drawer in his desk after taking a careful look at it."

"What is the law in such a case?"

"I don't think there is any precedent. Perhaps the publican should keep it a reasonable time. Finding of dangerous drugs should be reported, but on the other hand could Lane have reasonably known the danger? I much doubt whether you could get a conviction."

"I think I should ask Lane for a statement."

"Use care," said the Super. "He has Palabras behind him, and in spite of his eccentricities Sir Hugh has on occasion a set of very nasty teeth. I know he's always smiling at you, but sometimes you wonder . . . But to get back to my business. Hawker told me that Palabras might have some unauthorised documents in his possession. He was not forthcoming—any help from you?"

"A foolscap file containing eight hundred pieces of paper—various sizes and colours, stapled within. Marked on the outside in red ink: 'N775—A1—Ministerial Level'."

"Probably a report on the staff loos."

"More than that," said Harry, "but it's hidden away in a bank vault, so he says, and he impresses as a truthful man on matters of fact."

"You asked him!"

"Yes." The Chief Inspector felt himself colour.

"I retire next March," said the Super. "I suppose it is getting a bit beyond me. I believe Mr. Hawker is being given an even bigger computer. With that and a civil question to suspects as to whether they did it, no doubt we shall have a crime-free society and public libraries specialising in porn. Thank God that I shan't be around too long to see it."

They all got that way eventually, thought Harry. Progress out-stripped you unless you were very nippy on your pins, like Hawker. The punch cards nurtured you, gathered you up, and finally discarded you, squalling, like an ungrateful old mum.

"There was no point in searching his house for the file," he said aloud. "With his resources Palabras has a thousand ways to hide it. I dare say he could have it smuggled abroad."

The Super's dentures gyrated and he pushed the remainder of the cucumber sandwiches, though somewhat wistfully, away and took a soda mint with the remainder of the tea.

"Eventually we'll have to gloss over Miss Sloper," he opined. "Young vandals out at nights with guns—we have had plenty of complaints from the farmers, a sow was shot through the head only last month."

Cucumber generally played up with the Chief Inspector and it did now. It was only when he had peeped into the public bar of the Marquis of Tenterton that he remembered that Honeybody was not there. Lane was not at the reception desk: the dismal porter on duty said that the gaffer might be in his office.

The landlord was reading the evening paper and seemed

not pleased to see Harry. "Sorted it all out?" he asked. "I hope so because we are short of rooms."

Without being asked the Chief Inspector squeezed in front of the desk and sat down upon the battered kitchen chair. "Might be here some time, but it won't matter if your own room is rentable."

Lane's mouth made a sneering motion. "If you have a warrant, then execute it without the music-hall bit."

"I'll come to the point, Mr Lane. One of the barbiturate compounds in Title's brandy bottle was a rare French brand. A former chambermaid would testify that she handed some in to you. I must warn you that you are entitled not to comment: on the other hand an innocent person might want to make a statement."

Harry raised one knee against the desk as the burly publican half rose but the man only stretched his back and sank down again.

"I'll just tell you a little story that might not be true. A man had a son who became bitter politically and in fact did a bit of time for assaulting the police. There was a gang led by a violent man called Paddy Big Brain, a smart, wild man. The son joined Paddy: there was nothing the father could do about it. One night they raided a small explosive shed, and there the armed police were waiting. The gang got away, except for the man's son who died on the way to hospital. So, for the man, with no wife or other children, it was up stakes and a new life in England. One by one the gang died away. Paddy Big Brain was nursing a bomb when it went off, so maybe he was not the genius they said he was. But the father got a letter from one of them who had got away to the States. It said that the man who betrayed them on the night was an informer named Justin Title, a smooth-speakin' white worm who was now safe in England. It meant little. Let the dead bury their dead, but one day the father encountered a gabby, persuasive fellow named Justin Title. I—the man—was not unversed in drawing a man out, you do not spend your life dealing with the public without learning the art. It was the self-same Justin Title. Still, nothing happened, and he moved on. But a second time he came back and that was too much..."

"Are you saying you poisoned him, Mr. Lane?"

Lane meant to chuckle, but it was an unpleasant noise that emerged. "I was just spinnin' a little yarn about people who are dead and wouldn't give evidence if they were alive. Just what motive would you ascribe to me if you brought a case? French barbiturate! There are thousands of French coming here each year, and thousands of English goin' to Europe where some of the chemists, I'm told, aren't that fussy about prescriptions."

"It looks as though you'll get away with it," said Harry, pleasantly. "Title sounds a nasty bit of goods from whichever direction viewed."

"Pat me on the back, give me a cigar, and ask me to sign my name to a statement," gibed Lane.

"I've got two sons," said Harry, "and I know what you felt. Nevertheless, you know, we won't let you rest. The pressure becomes pretty hard to bear, and there is always the possibility, however remote, that a connecting link will come into our hands."

Lane neatly folded his paper. "Perhaps we can desist from this delightful conversation because I must be about my business."

"Title was prying into Sir Hugh's business! I suppose that could not be the motive for a faithful old servitor?"

"For a little fellah, you talk a lot," said Lane impassively, but Harry thought it wise to get out of the little office quickly. He went up to his bedroom and locked the door.

Chapter Five

Bosky Lane shot himself at seven o'clock the next morning, soon after making himself a cup of tea on the hot plate which stood in the alcove of his bedroom. The Chief Inspector became awake through the sounds of scurry. Eventually there was knocking and Honeybody's bashan-like voice exhorting him to get cracking for Christ's sake will you. There was no doubt that Lane had shot himself through the right temple—Harry had seen a dozen cases. The unpleasant position was unmistakable and the police surgeon later agreed.

"No note," said the local Superintendent after the corpse had been taken away. "Did you see him?"

"He denied poisoning Title." Harry did not wish to give chapter and verse. "He might have done so, but we can't bring that into an inquest."

"Unsound mind." The Super looked at the little doctor. "Were you treating him?"

"He was a nervous case. A lot of these big, stout men are. A worrier, I would guess. I had him on a diet, which seemed to improve matters, plus stuff for his stomach. He said, two days ago, that he rarely slept until around six, then when the alarm went off he felt hellish. Typical. He would not take sleeping pills, seemed to have a horror of 'em. Generally speaking he was organically very healthy for his age, blood pressure O.K. in spite of slight obesity. What's this about him poisoning people?"

"We thought he might have slipped the stuff into Justin Title's brandy bottle," said Harry.

"You won't prove it now. As the Super said, 'while of unsound mind'."

"A typical case," said Honeybody. "You wake up with a dry mouth and all your sins pressing on you. The old kings knew what was what when they always had a tot of wine on the bedhead."

"A cheap Belgian pistol," mourned the Super, "of the kind that was turned out in thousands for the Congo, as was. A million to one that we will never trace it."

"Well," said the doctor, "I'd better go and call on the living."

After he had gone the Super looked at Harry strangely. "It was sheer force of habit, but I glanced in the top drawer of his desk downstairs, vaguely thinking he might have left a note there." He opened his briefcase and produced an empty cardboard file, foolscap size, marked in red ink on the outside: 'N775—A1—Ministerial Level'.

"Your alley, I think," said the Super, not without malice. "I had my man do a quick check, but there seem to be no recognisable dabs."

"I'd like to borrow, say, three experienced searchers," said Harry. "Our masters will want fast action. Honeybody, you inform the Coroner's officer."

"I'll send three along," said the Super, placing the file on the unmade bed and obviously wanting to be out of the place. "Two are pretty experienced, the other one a beginner. But, Lord, it'll be like looking in a haystack." He went out with Honeybody.

The room had a small bathroom cum loo. Harry stood on tiptoe and saw that nothing was taped under the cistern cover or thrust under the bath. The underside of the mattress yielded nothing; equally bare were the top of the wardrobe and its back after the Chief Inspector had rocked it away from the wall. Remembering that Lane's desk had appeared cluttered, he noted with surprise that his personal possessions were almost unduly tidy. There was a laundry bag of soiled linen: the wardrobe smelled of dry-cleaning with seven conservatively cut suits, mostly wool. The shirts and underwear were immaculately folded. Lane apparently cleaned his own shoes, all assembled on 'trees'. No photographs, no books, a folded evening paper. An anonymous room.

Downstairs there were stares from the staff, but the pub functioned from momentum. The Chief had toast and coffee.

"How is the gaffer?" enquired the waitress.

"As well as can be expected."

"They say in the kitchen that he's corpsed."

"So he is." Harry put on his occasional ferocious glare and the woman flounced away.

The Super was as good as his word, for Harry had barely finished, conscious of the covert glances and whisperings of his fellow guests, when two elderly, sly-looking constables arrived plus a younger eager-beaver who was plainly intent on achieving great things. The senior man perfunctorily asked for instructions, and the Chief Inspector replied: "You know the job better than I do. It's the contents of a file—eight hundred pieces of paper, different sizes and colours. Plus any firearms or suspicious objects."

They were crowded into Lane's little office.

"It'll be a long job, no doubt," said the P.C. comfortably, aware of possible perquisites in the way of free beer. "We'd better start in here."

He could do no good and anyway he was only putting off the evil hour of telephoning Hawker. He did this from the sub-post-office hearing his superior's heavy breathing and the faint rustle of a tape recorder.

"At least we have the cover of that goddamned file," said

the old man at length. "Lane was the safe deposit that Palabras had in mind. There must have been a relationship of trust there. I checked on the publican yesterday and he was not a political animal. He had the reputation of being a first-class pub-keeper—came of a family of them—and was his own master at a small, licensed hotel near Cork when he chucked it up after his son died and came over here. The son was a mercurial type who got in with violent company. The father had the reputation of being a bit of a bully to his staff, so perhaps there was a streak of violence there. We have no record of how he came to know Palabras. Perhaps you should ask the good baronet," Hawker gave a sneering sniff. "What time did you go up to bed?"

"A quarter to ten, I guess."

"Suppose we take it that Lane got windy. He might well have had the file placed among his business records. He takes the papers out of the file so they take up less space. He either puts them somewhere, or else makes up a small package which he either put in a post-box or took round to Palabras personally."

"Can you do something about the post angle?"

Theoretically mail is sacrosanct except for the Customs, but there are ways if one pulls enough rank.

"Mr. Quarles will see to that. You and that fat Sergeant, Um—" Hawker rarely admitted to knowing Honeybody's name—"check on whether he went out of the pub and if possible where to, and for God's sake get a move on—you know what the press is going to do to us. 'The Angel of Death hovers over the quiet village of Waddington Parva' is what one of them said yesterday. Now it'll be two ruddy Angels, or maybe a bloody-minded Seraph, at it."

"Perhaps." Harry knew how to infuriate Hawker.

"And don't send in reports looking like a dog's dinner," bawled his superior as he slammed down the handset.

He was unpleasantly certain that the old sub-post-mistress who was glittering at him through her glasses had in some way overheard the conversation, but maybe it was nerves. Emerging he nearly collided with Honeybody who was accompanied by a man who looked like a lecherous rabbit but proved to be the Coroner's officer. The Chief Inspector noted a faint whiff of brandy in the air. "Cold work in the morgue," forestalled Honeybody, "with all that ice, so me and Mr. Thye had a warming drop, him living locally."

"Ar," said Mr. Thye, "that it is and what with three violent deaths and four peaceful ones from the Institution, fallen out of bed, they 'ave to buy ice from the fishmonger so that they don't Turn, like. Coroner is doing one Justin Title at noon, open verdict it'll be, and poor Miss Sloper at six, which means overtime. He'll probably get round to the publican tomorrow afternoon."

"I don't think there is any need for you to go to the morgue, Sergeant." Honeybody became chap-fallen, but the Coroner's assistant, sensitive to atmosphere, beamed a good-bye and crossed the road at a rapid clip.

"A nice fellow," remarked the Sergeant. "I've noticed those connected with morgues generally are."

"Did you learn anything last night?"

"It's not a large town, said Honeybody. "A ten-pub, one off-licence country town with no decent grub to be had at nights. But Miss Sloper was known there: most of the people from this village shop at Granchester. She did, and of course there were the Guides and the Blankets for Old People Fund meeting every Tuesday. She used to take her lunch at the best of the pubs, the Dragon, when she went over. I had a bit of an introduction from the barmaid at the Marquis. Her cousin is the potman. No, Miss Sloper wasn't liked at all. Nosy and bossy!"

"Did Title frequent Granchester?"

"He did not and I got no report whatsoever of sinister strangers asking questions."

A penny dropped. "I've been a fool," said Harry as they walked along. "Title was an Irish police informer, Miss Sloper was Intelligence, probably too smart for her own good. It is quite reasonable to suppose that she knew of Title. He never changed his name, probably on the assumption that it is more dangerous to fake a new identity than to brazen out a true one. She contacted Title. Look, I'll tell you what happened between Lane and me last night..."

When he had finished, Honeybody said shrewdly: "Lane was pretty adept at watching and surmising, so I've been told. He already had his son's death marked on the ledger. If he gathered that Title was after Palabras, that might have been the last straw. But he was not a murderous type and when you taxed him with it he could not bear it any more. He was probably a mixed-up type at bottom."

The Chief Inspector had never got calloused and he winced, glad to see the portico of the Marquis of Tenterton. Obviously fired by ambition the porter rubbed his hands in a kind of false genuflection and whispered, with fruity breath, that Sir Hugh Palabras was in the private dining-room and would like to see them. "I'm *temprary* hin charge 'ere."

On the ground floor, the private dining-room was something of an Edwardian relic, with stuffed fish in glass cases and a long table fit to sit twenty people. It was adorned by a long, dismal-green cloth with tassels on which stood two bowls of wax fruit. It smelled of disuse. At the head of the table sat Sir Hugh, a trifle pale this morning.

"This room has not been used these forty years," he said after greetings. "Poor Lane was always on to me about it, wanting a snack bar, but I never got round to it. Why did he suicide?"

"It was pretty plain that he poisoned Justin Title's brandy, though we could probably not have proved it. Title informed on Lane's son, who was shot in Ireland."

"I met Lane one day near Cork," said Sir Hugh. "A bad rainy day and I wanted lunch. I was at a loose end and here was this lovely little hotel with fish caught a few hours ago and cooked perfectly. Finally, I stayed the night. There was nobody else there in January and I had a good crack with Lane, the landlord, who must have been fortyish then. Years later, I got a letter asking if I had perhaps a vacancy for a pub manager. You will be aware that I own the local brewery. He explained that he had lost his only child. It happened that the Marquis of Tenterton was in difficulties owing to a bad landlord, so it was quite a godsend. Lane did very well for me. I liked him personally: we thought alike, so it seemed, and he was content with his lot."

"Was he a bullying person?" asked Harry.

You became aware that Sir Hugh's constant smile was some kind of nervous rictus. It froze on him now. "He may have liked to throw his weight about, but staff are difficult and pub-running has problems."

"The cover of your file was in his desk."

"My file?"

"The one from the F.O."

"I told you truthfully that it was not in my house, nor is it now."

"But Lane had it in custody?"

"You must work that out yourselves. The porter tells me that you have men searching here. On what authority?"

"None really. Your brewery could get an injunction, perhaps even a local warrant for tresspass," said Harry slowly, "if you wanted that kind of publicity."

"You know damn well I don't." Sir Hugh had recovered himself. "I trusted Lane... at certain times I asked him to carry out confidential errands for me. He had no interest in politics, barring a deep dislike of Westminster, not a hard thing to achieve. I suppose he had a brainstorm."

"Things obviously got too much for him. We won't keep you any longer, Sir Hugh."

They went to Honeybody's room. "He was a bit twisty," said the Sergeant. "There's an old fire-escape door at the back. Lane could have slipped out and delivered the papers if he had made up his mind to do away with himself."

"Palabras was at a speaking engagement in Bournemouth," said Harry. "At least there was a par. in the evening paper that he was going to speak about Japan."

"I got the impression," said Honeybody, "that Sir H. did not like his tenants. But my barlady—she don't like barmaid—says they are fairly thick. Old Señor Abajo, General Gould and Mrs. Peremely-Fox, Dr. Tulkingham—Sir Hugh has the right of bestowing the living, or had until they altered advowsons—old Bruggles, the ham actor: only Miss Sloper was really on the outer, they all hating her. A lovely little nest, when you look at it coldly. The Government's favourite general, his political niece, an old Spaniard with no whatsits who knew everybody in Europe in his time, the world's finest tragedian (see the adverts) and sneaking Sloper, as the girls used to call her. Old Tulkingham flogs stuffed Whimbles through the *Observer*. What a lovely cover! Stuff 'em with dope or stolen documents. Who looks into a Whimble? Like that fellow who sells women through the *Times Literary Supplement*."

"We watched the Vicar stuffing," said the Chief Inspector mildly, "and he was using sawdust and a forcing bag. But I suppose it's an idea. If Palabras's machinations needed it, I suppose the interior of a Whimble is as cunning a place as you could think of. Palabras has a mint of money and a vast if vague ambition and sense of destiny. If you can hide secret papers in a pumpkin, inside a stuffed Whimble is merely a progression. The tenants on the Estate all seem to have certain weaknesses, even if you have to include old Abajo's lusting after exotic dishes. I wonder if Sloper was a double agent!"

"But all those years in the Service!" Honeybody was aghast.

"Use your brains," snapped Harry. "The records abound with such histories. Often it is a corrupt desire for power, sometimes disillusion. If you spend twenty years amid the double-cross, the treble-cross *ad infinitum,* your sense of value gets a bit addled. She approached Title with an offer for the papers, Lane murdered Title, perhaps because Palabras dropped a hint that the man was dangerous to this snug little feudal domain, and then somebody killed Sloper who knew too much. I thought at one time it might not be so, but I think somebody meant to get Sloper, and that means a first-class marksman."

The telephone rang. It was Hawker. "No postal packets of the kind to hold the documents were posted in Waddington Parva last night," he said crisply. "You can take that for solid fact."

"I want to see Gough Trengold who originally took the file," said Harry. "I suppose he's on duty today."

Paper rustled. "Yes," said Hawker, "with two men watching him. He lunches late these days, about five past two, a Scotch and a beef sandwich at a pub called Dove's in Old Angel Street. You have his photo—sallow-faced fellow who dyes his hair black. I'll warn you that you won't get anything from him unless you have discovered a new way to open oysters."

"It's worth a try. Sergeant Honeybody can attend the inquest on Title. I'll get the ten-thirty train from Granchester."

"I got a teletype," grunted Hawker, "and they have not found the gun which killed Miss Sloper."

"It might be inside a Whimble" said Harry.

"A Whimble?"

"The Vicar stuffs 'em," said the Chief Inspector and did not stay for an answer, merely cautioning Honeybody not to appear drunk at the Coroner's Court—a habit of his—before rousing the driver of Waddington Parva's one taxi, who mysteriously earned a living by dozing over the *Sporting Life* and letting the back seat out to those euphemistically called courting couples. He was not pleased at the prospect of driving the four miles to Granchester and doubted that the motor would start. Harry said it had bloody well better, and the ancient vehicle wheezed off. By his rank the Chief Inspector was entitled to First Class where the grime was less and the 1900 scenic photographs of Bournemouth bore faded hand-colouring.

Taking time off to phone his wife, who seemed bored, he got to Dove's just before two. Old Angel Street was in reality a narrow alley abutting mews and Dove's had obviously at one time served the coachmen. Nowadays it was dark, comfortable, with small booths, a pile of good sandwiches and a regular clientèle. He ordered a sandwich and glass of bitter and was halfway through when Gough Trengold entered and exchanged a brief nod with the regulars. It was a small place and the Chief Inspector had strategically placed himself so that a newcomer would naturally stand next to him, at least to order.

More difficult than it theoretically seems, matching people

to photographs is one of the minor police arts. In fact the sardonic depth of Trengold's expression did not get through the lens. It was accentuated by the greenish tinge of his eyes, which were expressionless as Harry said: "Mr. Gough Trengold?"

"Yes, but I don't know you."

"We have mutual acquaintances, no doubt, but there is an empty booth."

Trengold seemed in his element. He took his change and preceded the Chief Inspector into the narrow-gutted booth —Victorian coachmen must have been lank and thin, thought Harry momentarily as his belly slid along the edge of the dark oak fixed table. He took a card out of his wallet. Trengold did not pick it up: merely glanced down. "Keep it for another occasion, Mr. James, we civil servants hating waste. If you are on expenses, you may soon buy me another whisky, which is merely sustenance."

"A pleasure, though I must say my card usually provides food enough for thought without the addition of Scotch."

Trengold lit a small, black cigar, showing yellowed teeth as he did so. "Mr. James—let us forget titles as I am myself a Senior Clerk, third division and clean and pensionable—a file was missing from the office I work in. Since which time I have been pestered, badgered, shadowed, had it offered free by obviously professional tarts, had my correspondence cunningly opened, and my telephone emit a curious gurgling noise when I took the receiver off quickly. A good, honest Yardman is a refreshing change from the pismires who have been shadowing me."

Dove's was not Trengold's first port of call, thought Harry. There was a slight tremor in the man's hand as he drained his drink. The Chief Inspector got another from the bar.

"You are nervous, Mr. Trengold."

"You'd be a little nervous if you got the impression that

people with bowler hats were peering at you out of telephone boxes."

"Why not just come clean?"

"Because I am innocent. Secondly because I shall be pensioned off in five years' time and that is what I shall have to live on in very modest comfort, but it is a damned sight better than not ever being able to afford a glass of comfort or a smoke."

"Palabras looks after friends."

"I know nothing of Palabras except common report."

"It's murder, now, Mr. Trengold."

A spot of whisky slopped off on to Trengold's grey lapel. He rubbed it with a forefinger. "Palabras... murdered!"

"A tenant of his who was interested in the file. Believe me, Mr. Trengold, you seem to have set some rather crude violence in action."

"I am not a man of violence. Who was murdered?"

"A Miss Sloper, an ex-Intelligence-Officer probably turned rogue."

"What do you want of me?"

"Suppose you just have a yarn to me in strictest confidence."

"I suppose you are carrying two bugs and have a small pard under the table with a notebook." Trengold peered at his feet.

"For an educated man," said Harry, "you don't seem to know much about the Law of Evidence. If you keep to generalities, a chat cannot hurt you. Mind you, if you give me solid facts I shall have to try to prove them. But why not talk a bit? Lord love us, it would be easy for the Establishment to give you a bit of a kick upstairs and retire you early on full pension. They'll watch you as a matter of course, no avoiding that, and I would not personally apply for a passport renewal, but say a snug little retirement this coming year..."

"Generalities only," said Trengold.

"Why did you do it?"

"You know how long I've worked for the effers. 'Oh, Trengold,'" he went into falsetto, "'they want those documents on Inja by noon. Sort them out, there's a good feller.' Marlborough School, teeth and temper, double firsts and the brains of an ant, the cruelty of a tiger. Palabras is the hope of the country, it's stood out for years. Wipe out the muck and start again, or else become a minor Portugal. O.K., suppose I decided to give Palabras something explosive... No money was passed, I assure you of that!"

"Odd altruism," commented Harry. "I've always thought I would need a heavy bribe."

"Typical Establishment," said Trengold, "but you know the rhyme about the British journalist and bribery—'there is really not much reason to'. It applies to the Civil Service at middle grade. We hate the bastards."

"It clears up a point or two," said the Chief Inspector, "but leaves a slight perplexity. Other people are trying to nab that file, and I cannot for the life of me see how they would know."

Trengold's odd-looking eyes wbecame slits of malice. "I wanted to stir things up perhaps, so I sent little letters to certain Embassies and Consulates. Suppose that! Mind you, I am just making an intelligent guess. And what about buying me one for it?"

Harry did, together with two ham sandwiches, one of which he took for himself.

"Your hours and drinking seem flexible," he commented.

"Pariahs have privileges, old chap. If they fired me it would, as you just surmised, be possibly inconvenient. Much easier to brush me under the elegant Axminster which my boss has acquired by years of bum-buttering."

"I suppose you knew the contents of the file?"

"The swine have to have confidential *clurks* to file the documents of perfidy. I dare say Himmler had hundreds of them, documenting and filing away. Why they do it, God alone knows! If you committed a murder you wouldn't hire several clerks and a filing cabinet! I know the sordid details of several hundred sell-outs and a massacre or two. The file you keep referring to deals with when . . ."

"Shut up," said Harry taking up his hat. He left Trengold sitting there, a sly leer on his face.

Hawker would be in Whitehall until four, so the Chief Inspector telephoned and found that Dianile Higgins had returned to her elegant little Hampstead apartment. She showed no enthusiasm, but remarked that she was in for the afternoon, still feeling shaken up, and if he called she could give him fifteen minutes at most, providing it was before five o'clock. The departmental report had said 'elegant' and was completely right, for Miss Higgins existed in what was basically one of those elegant boxes which often belie the quality of the chocolates within. No maid, thought Harry looking around. Miss Higgins wore a yellow pyjama suit which would have flattered her better if she had been half a stone lighter, and was having an afternoon coffee. She did not offer the Chief Inspector one.

"I thought we got this over the other day," she said, seating herself on a chair which was worth plenty if genuine.

Without being asked the Chief Inspector chose an inconvenient, low Spanish stool.

"Only one question. Why did Title undertake this assignment? I mean it was a bit out of character, because of recent years he had got a nice easy connection without violence. The kind of thing he put his nose into reeks of violence quite often."

"Justin had had some little misunderstanding with his fellow countrymen a few years ago. He couldn't go back for fear of being, well, shot, though he was safe here as they don't like to foul the English nest very much if they can help it. His old friends heard about certain papers that Palabras was sitting on. They thought he'd do a secret deal with Whitehall to return them—the Governorship of Australia or some such thing. They wanted them published—anywhere. They got word to Justin that if he could fix it, the past would be forgotten. Of course, there was money in it, too. Justin thought it an admirable opportunity." There were fat tears marring her make-up.

"Do you know who he was going to flog the documents to?"

She shrugged. "They were hot and worth money. He thought the Americans would jump at them . . . apparently they were in on whatever it was, but Justin thought the East Germans would pay in Swiss currency. It was the opportunity of his lifetime. Oh, God! It was his lifetime."

The Chief Inspector let himself out and went by bus to Scotland Yard and Superintendent Hawker who glared at him.

Harry gave him the cover of the file.

"They tell me the only way to lose weight is not to eat or drink," grumbled the old Superintendent, "and if that's not unpleasant enough I get bloody fools giving me bits of cardboard." He sighed. "I got on to your fat Sergeant fifteen minutes ago. Title was brought in as suicide while of unsound mind and'll be interred tomorrow. The Marquis of

Tenterton has as yet not yielded the documents and the gun that killed the woman has not been found. The only thing I have done, while you were fooling about up here, is to get permission for search warrants for the Palabras, Gould, Abajo and the actor fellow's houses. Sheer self-protection. The Home Office has been giving me hell. Why no arrest? I got the impression that they wouldn't care who we arrested as long as it would shut the press up."

"Trengold admitted to me in confidence that he sent the papers to Palabras, for no reason other than mischief, received no payment and broadcast the anonymous fact to sundry Embassies and organisations. Title was approached by Irish 'friends' to expedite the distribution of the documents."

"The Government is worried," said Hawker. "A worried politician is a dangerous man to us bureaucrats." For the moment he looked human.

"I wondered if Palabras was shrewd enough to give only the file cover to the publican," said Harry. "It would be a nice piece of misdirection."

Hawker rubbed his nose. "I am inclined to think that Palabras was honest with you to an extent. On the principle that the simpler solution is probably the correct one I would imagine that Lane had the entire file. Then when he decided to shuffle off, he removed the contents, folded or rolled them in a small package and disposed of it. Nothing except letters and a few aerograms went into Waddington Parva post boxes last evening—Quarles got it checked. This morning the Vicar's wife posted ten large packages, but one supposes she is Caesar's wife."

"He sells stuffed birds. I suppose one could conceal anything in the stuffing."

"That's your Sergeant's evil imagination," said Hawker, "you haven't got the gift... I have personally arrested seven vicars, but mostly about boys. I should not imagine that the Vicar deals in questionable documents."

"He is indebted to Palabras and old General Gould for the living. My Sergeant says that Palabras carries a lot of weight."

Hawker snorted. "A surprising number of men and women have ruined themselves because they became fascinated by Palabras. There are men like that and God knows what they have got. You'd better wait until the result of the search parties comes in."

It came in in half an hour's time, the interim spent by Harry in drinking interminable cups of tea in the canteen. He was summoned to the briefing room, where Hawker waited before the loudspeaker.

In the event the Vicar's house had been searched as well, the reverend gentleman apparently having been quite pleased to expose the interior of the Whimbles on his working bench and loquacious on the subject of Rendering to Caesar, personified by two sergeants brought in from Bournemouth. General Gould had babbled of Civil Rights until his niece shut him up. Old Señor Abajo had slept peacefully, but Chef Beedle had muttered about Afro Unity. Bruggles's house had yielded a surprising collection of pornography and a youngish man with a dubious passport.

"Believed to be one John Smith," declaimed the anonymous voice of the announcer, "probably born in Limerick and reputedly a forger of literary items—letters, signatures, bits of manuscript. Aged around thirty-two and made a killing over a Henry James diary in nineteen sixty-eight when he went to live in Palma de Mallorca with an American passport listing him as Tomas de Lisle. He planted a forged map alleged to be by Columbus's Sailing Master on to the Smithsonian Institute who eventually smelled a rat—for which they had paid seventy thousand dollars. He is a very clever, adept and academically wise forger. Bruggles was his friend and when the Spanish police started an investigation, prodded by Interpol, he fled with Bruggles intending to lie low. Of course, he denied the forgery. It is now over to the F.B.I. if they want to take action, all sales having been made to the States as far as we know."

"Is there any suggestion that the documents in the case were forged?" asked Harry.

"They came from the Foreign Office files," snapped Hawker.

"Is that the answer?"

"Look, son, it's an answer for us poor mortals. And the man forges Henry James and Ibsen—hardly a pattern of Home Office style, which is a mixture of Edgar Wallace and constipation."

The Chief Inspector thought for a while. Then he said: "You can forge a whole wad of stuff, as Ireland did in his Shakespeare forgeries, but you eventually find a shrewd old scholar who spots something that throws you flat on your face. The better way is little bits of touching up which make a humdrum document turn into something exciting and valuable. If Palabras is going to cause a stir with those documents, he might want to have the lily gilded a little. Still, one feels that Palabras would not stoop to forgery . . ."

"Nonsense, he's a politician. Keep the possibility in mind."

Everything was easier said than done, ruminated the Chief Inspector the following morning, after a night spent listening to the whining of his twin sons, who had contracted mumps, and the inevitable complaints from his wife and they never seemed to take a holiday, when the people next door—and he on a meagre wage—incessantly flew to Torremolinos.

These dismal memories were fortified by the five o'clock train to Granchester which, as a gloating porter informed him, had been wrecked the previous Saturday by football fans so that, God strike him if he told a lie, there wasn't a comfortable berth for anybody's arse in the whole lot of carriages. For once British Rail was right, and Harry spent much of the time stretching his legs amidst the bits of old sandwiches in the corridor and looking gloomily at the scrawls about the Tory Government and the wrongs of Ireland. The day was watery when he got off the bus at Waddington Parva, but he decided not to go to the Marquis of Tenterton, which besides probable disorganisation also contained Honeybody, whose cheerful presence he felt he could not abide. Instead he went into a place labelled the 'Tea Tree Inne' as the church clock inaccurately struck eight thirty. Four old ladies in pea-green miniskirts were laying tables and to the gruffest of these Harry conveyed his desire for breakfast.

"It's only teas and you're a bit early for that," said the old lady, in upper-class accent.

"A strong brew of tea and the inevitable buttered scone, then."

"We could do an egg I suppose," the old lady said with condescension. "Hilda, have we an egg?"

"I think there is one," scowled another old lady.

It proved almost as elderly as its erstwhile owners, and as hard-boiled, but the Chief Inspector ate it plus the plastic scone, for which he was apparently expected to pay off the mortgage on the shop.

"On expenses are you not?" leered the head old lady as she made change. "We pay rates and taxes to support the police, who go around in the lap of luxury."

"I didn't know my profession stood out so clearly."

"Miss Sloper was part-owner of our tea-room."

"What was she like?"

"She'd been in the Forces," said the old lady as if it explained everything, "and she didn't like the civilians. We are all Forces' widows here."

"I suppose you know General Gould?"

"He never tips—we are not above taking a gratuity"—the old lady eyed Harry's change and he found himself making calculations as to twelve and a half per cent: she looked as if she would scorn his usual ten—"but generals are generals, as we know."

"No idea who killed her?" Harry scooped up the remainder of his change.

"It must have been Chef Beedle, no woman being safe from the blacks."

"I didn't think they shot them through the head."

"In my thirty-five years in the Punjab I never ventured out of the bungalow." The old lady's mouth set rat-trap. "You mark my words, where there's mischief, there's a black."

"What about the Irish?" enquired Harry, by now fascinated.

"We are Irish." The old lady was distinctly hostile. "Are you not aware that the English Forces, at any rate at the higher ranks, are Irish gentlemen?"

Harry smirked and fled, the plastic scone heavy upon his colon. In spite of the light rain it was one of the fresh, clear English mornings, with the sloping main street of Waddington Parva and the thatched roofs of the houses below the village (the smell from the broken sewer-pipe being fortunately invisible), making a scene like a tourist postcard. By now the Chief Inspector had committed to memory the intricacies of the paths traversing the Palabras Estate. He was making his way when a querulous voice behind a clump of yew trees whined: "It's only worth forty pounds as meat."

"You couldn't let that London gent ride him, sir," said a

bucolic voice. "He falls down on the slightest provocation and faints if he sees a fence. It's not the gent, sir. To break 'is neck he's right welcome by yours truly. But the 'unt, sir, it gives an 'unt a bad name when too many break their necks and you get the subscriptions falling off sadly. Let the 'ounds 'ave 'im, sir, not that there's much meat on him."

"You know the price of feed as well as I do." It was General Gould in a bad mood, or perhaps a usual mood, realised Harry, as he went round the trees.

An elderly, cunning rustic in whipcord breeches, probably the Huntsman, was holding the bridle of a withered old chestnut, which might indeed have fallen over had not the rustic leant heavily against him.

"Sell him, General," counselled Mrs. Peremely-Fox, "it's *caveat emptor*, and one hundred and fifty pounds." She was intimidating in slacks and a short duffle coat.

"Morning, sir, morning, madam," falsely smiled the Chief Inspector. "Trouble with the 'osses?"

"An ethical problem," snarled the General. "All my life I have been plagued by them. The Service is full of ethical problems, as I am outlining in my autobiography, 'Hitting Them for Six'. Dealing with Wogs, of course, clears your mind and you realise that you must not get soft, as I tell the Americans. Williams!"

"Sir!" said the Huntsman, exuding a whiff of cloves overlaying beer.

"Tell Mr. Forrest that he can have the chestnut, with no veterinary guarantee," the General raised his eyes as if for Divine Guidance, "for two hundred and fifty pounds cash. See you have a respectable witness. Dr. Tulkingham will do the job: I'll get him to be pottering around within earshot. If Mr. Forrest refuses, feed it to the dogs. How old is it?"

"When you bought 'im for the 'unt, sir, you said 'e was

ten, which would make 'im sixteen. But the teeth, sir, such as 'e's got, look about fifty to me."

"That'll do. Trot him off."

Horse and Huntsman lurched away along the path, while the General fingered his scrappy moustache.

"Have to take what we can get nowadays, Chief Inspector, particularly anything to do with horses."

"In the old days," said Mrs. Peremely-Fox, agog, "the General would have lashed him for impertinence."

"He gets thirty pounds a week," said General Gould, "and a flat above the stables. But drunk or not he doesn't actually fall off. The other one we had kept pawing the ladies when helping them through gates and falling off his horse after the Hunt Breakfast, though I now provide only lemonade."

"You're not attending the inquest on Miss Sloper? ... no reason why you should," said Harry.

"It would be morbid curiosity," said Mrs. Peremely-Fox, "and I suppose we would not be permitted to View the Body, not being invited to participate on the Jury, though one would expect that at least the General would have been approached."

"Seen a lot of corpses in my time," observed the General with a kind of shy pride. "Nothing to me. But have you arrested the man who killed her?"

"The locals haven't even found the gun, some kind of precision target rifle it is supposed to have been."

"I never held with fancy rifles," said the General. "Cold steel was what we made our reputation by."

"And keeping people in their proper places, which was the making of the Empah whichever way you look at it," interposed his niece.

"It was a pretty good piece of shootin' by all accounts," admitted the General with expertise, "and I suppose it would have been impracticable to bayonet the old cow."

"Any idea who did it?"

"That black chef," said Mrs. Peremely-Fox. "I cannot sleep quietly in my bed thinking of black men around the Estate."

"Somebody has to do the work," said the General. "I had a bit of impudence from my batman the other day when the bathroom got stopped up. I told him I'd get a nigger to do the work if I had more of that talk. Probably the black chef did it: she doubtless resisted his advances and he did her in like that fellow in Shakespeare. Well, I have work today and my niece has to take her place on the Bench."

"Incest is rife in Waddington Parva," said Mrs. Peremely-Fox, "and must be put down or it will spread like wildfire."

Harry pushed on to the house of Bruggles. This time the curtains were drawn, and the theatrical knight opened the front door with a glove and secateurs in his left hand.

"Um," he said.

"Chief Inspector Harry James, though I don't particularly mind being called Um."

"Of course I remember," lied Bruggles, "though one meets so many people, m'dear fellow. Come in, come in, the tea is being brewed in the kitchen. It is hard living, but the staff from London don't come for three days—I order them on contract, a lot of them members of the Profession now times are so hard. Good butlers, bad cooks, and the worst chambermaids are the Restoration actresses, sluts to a girl."

"Mr. Smith, I presume," Harry said to the short, squat, sallow-faced man brewing tea. He had a quick attractive smile and a voice which might have originated anywhere.

"Police, *I* presume?" said Smith. "I suppose a higher echelon than those we saw this morning."

"James from the Yard."

"Sounds like a butler."

"Well, when hanging was in vogue I was always deputed

to bring in the final breakfast, though, of course, it's a century since a forger was turned off."

"I say!" protested Bruggles.

"No trouble, my dear," said Smith. "No offence meant or taken, to coin a phrase. Oh, yes, I am a forger of sorts, giving innocent satisfaction to a number of people in return for a modest livelihood. No harm is done and one supposes that this gentleman knows that eighteen per cent of our historical documents are in fact forgeries."

"Do you do political documents?" asked Harry, accepting a cup of, this time, excellent tea.

"That is rather specialised," said the man known as John Smith. "I could do the actual handwriting part—and there is quite a lot to that—but the factual material would have to be provided. I'm literary and cartography basically—I could do you a little Ruskin note to his wife for ten pounds, taking me an hour and a little thought."

"Are you over here on a job?"

"I'm always working," said Smith, "and this is such a fertile field even though the American suckers are falling off, but the answer to the political question is quite definitely 'no'."

"Did you know Miss Sloper?"

"The woman who was shot? Not to the best of my knowledge. My cards are on the table. Things are a bit hot for me—I don't suppose any of the marks will care to give evidence because they are 'experts'. Nevertheless the Spanish police were nosing around my place in the Plaza Mayor in Madrid, and it was a time to lie low. My old friend here gave me hospitality."

More to it than that, thought the Chief Inspector. Smith obviously knew something about the actor.

"Thank you for a very good cup of tea," he said, and went in quest of Chef Beedle, who in the darkness of the hallway momentarily gave the impression of being a large, hairy poodle.

"The Chief Inspector," said Beedle without inflexion.

"Is Señor Abajo up and about?"

"The Señor is having breakfast in the sun room. I dressed him fifteen minutes ago."

Abajo looked more shrivelled than Harry remembered. He was propped up in a cane chair before a large glass window. Central heating made the room stifling.

"I cannot bear this cold," complained the old man. "You are the police inspector, no?"

Harry said he was, watching Abajo smear olive oil on to a piece of bread. Black coffee and what he thought was a tiny slug of anis stood on the little table. Abajo smiled, his crumpled face strangely lighting with mischief. "The peasant boy cannot avoid his early habits. Once, when I used to spend the long weekends in England—days long ago—the breakfasts were torture to me. Bacon!" The Spaniard gave a delicate shudder. "But it seems to me that we had police here yesterday. They searched for a gun and enquired about some papers. Of course, I have neither."

"The papers are purloined documents of State, Señor. You will appreciate the importance of this."

Abajo finished his morsel of bread and with one gulp downed the contents of the tiny glass. "English cooks are always horrified at my preferences, but the good Beedle acquiesces. Of course, his grandfather no doubt ate people on the sly. Yes, I heard something of these documents. I have not got them. I find myself at an age when dissimulation has no attraction, so I will tell you that I do not like the British Government."

"I wonder you live here."

"My dear Inspector, I should be in Andalucia with the sun seeping into my bones, but for the fact that I was and am a Republican. Your Government encourages the regime I detest, therefore I have no love for them. If your Westminster were abolished, I should rejoice, and if my old friend Palabras, whom I remember when he was at school, does this I shall die happy. Nevertheless I do not know the whereabouts of the documents."

"It is a question of three deaths."

"Death does not mean much to me."

"Was not Miss Sloper a friend?"

"No. She did not fit into our community. I thought she was an agent."

"For what?" In spite of himself, Harry sensed his voice sharpening.

Abajo looked younger by the minute, as he gathered the scarlet dressing-gown closer around his frail, shrunken chest.

"The world is filled with agents, Señor Policeman. If they do not want to sell you mail-order knitting machines, they desire to report your political opinions to the police. Of course I come from a country where the national occupation is spying on your neighbours, who in turn spy on you, and I recognised the tendency in Miss Sloper. I would imagine one of the agencies in the country desired to have reports about Sir Hugh, who is very dangerous, I think."

"He does not seem dangerous."

"Dangerous people never do. The blustering type often do not do anything. Do you find as a policeman that the meek little man is the one who cuts his wife up and cements her under the floor? I myself had occasion to poison my master and I was no bravo, no 'good boy' as we say in Andaluc', merely the meek and mild musician, solace to his declining years, which, however," Señor Abajo chuckled, "did not appear to me to be declining as fast as they might."

"You must have been a wit in your time, sir."

Something reptilian flickered momentarily behind the

Spaniard's almond eyes. "When you get to my age the wit is ingoing, rather than outgoing, because talking becomes an effort."

"No idea who killed Miss Sloper?"

"My only information comes from the good Beedle—I use the adjective because one of his oddly hirsute ears is undoubtedly glued against the door—but it would seem to point to a professional assassin, perhaps employed by the police. She may have been double-crossing your Masters, but now if you do not mind..." Before the old man's hand reached the little, portable bell-push, Chef Beedle entered, pointedly opening the door for Harry, who bowed and went out.

There was a savoury smell in the hallway and he remarked on it.

Chef Beedle had been looking sullen, but brightened at the culinary mention. "Pig's tripes," he said, "with chick peas. Beautiful, but inflates him with wind. We turn the radio up high when the Vicar calls for a chat, though the old gennelman's Catholic, of course, as much as he is anything."

"Do you get much mail?"

"Lots, nearly all foreign," Beedle paused at the front door. "The Señor knew very many people, a lot of them much younger. They write or send presents. Today there were three letters and a seed catalogue."

"No packets?"

"Nothing of that nature." Chef Beedle drew open the door.

"Something has been niggling at my mind," said Harry, suddenly. "You told me that you had been here for eight months, whereas I have reason to believe it is only six."

Massive shoulders shrugged and brown eyes surveyed the Chief Inspector without expression.

"In a rural area like this time just glides past. I may have said eight, but as I think of it it is six and two weeks. It is of no importance, sir. I had no intent to deceive."

Harry trudged back the way he had come. A girl in red was coming the other way. It was Miss Stinting, looking trim and expensive, her black curly hair perfectly groomed above the baby face.

"How's the shooting season?" she gibed.

A saucy bitch, thought Harry as he gave his most charming smile. "You did not contribute much."

"I told you a bod clobbered me." He noticed she carried a string bag lined with plastic. "It's a sole for the Master's lunch," she mimicked. "They have to be bought specially in Granchester because he thinks they are fresh in each day—so they are, by way of Aberdeen." She laughed to share the joke.

"What do you know about Chef Beedle?"

"Only what's on file, Mr. James. A Trotskyite, a good cook, and politically an activist which means he would readily plant plastic explosive under a cinema seat. I think things got too hot for him and he is down here to lie low. He's a wonderful cook, at least I heard Sir Hugh, who cossets his guts, drooling over a dinner Abajo had given, not that the old gentleman himself eats much except a little dago muck."

"He's been here six months and some days."

Miss Stinting's wide-set green eyes were contracted as she thought. "That would be right. He came to this village a month before me."

"When first I met him he gave me to believe he had been here eight months, in other words *before* the file was purloined. That seemed to whitewash him, Trotskyite or not. As it stands he applied for the job a month *after* it went off which puts an entirely different complexion on the matter."

She swung the string bag and the soles did not smell very

fresh. Noticing his expression she said: "Palabras goes in for very pungent sauces: his taste buds are nearly shot. But Beedle had no gun, or so he reported," she said with a needling sneer.

Harry momentarily contemplated rape, but the presence of Sir Hugh's lunch made it feel faintly sordid, so he kept his smile and said greasily: "The houses were searched with no results, likewise the grounds. I am sure that Beedle had no gun, just as I am sure you didn't. Either of you could have hidden it in a tree and come back later, but it is doubtful one supposes."

She was amused. "Oh, I didn't shoot Sloper, darling. You have been reading sensational literature. Actually the only thing I ever did was to kick a Russian cipher clerk in the shins and that was at a party. You have to kick Russians in the shins at parties. Have you thought of the Vicar?"

"Good God, not seriously."

"Funny people around," she said off-handedly. "Old Gould, still wildly ambitious to subdue Ireland or something. Gladys Peremely-Fox basically wanting to be the sadistic governor of a men's gaol, old Abajo living only to see Spain in some state of anarchy, Bruggles so beset with a lifetime of misdeeds and blackmail that he would do almost anything to get off the hook, and Dr. Tulkingham, who despises Christians but loves money. If you know how you can dismantle a rifle into quite small parts, except maybe the barrel which can go down a drain. He could have got rid of the small bits inside his stuffed birds. He's a good shot, at least with a shotgun, and accompanies Sir Hugh to his annual week of grouse-shooting. He brings back baskets filled with the wretched corpses and flogs them to the local fishmongers, though officially they are for nourishing broth for needy children. Well, if I don't get these soles home even Sir H.'s jaded palate will rebel." She wiggled past Harry, chucked him under the chin, and made off in a smell of old sole and expensive perfume.

It was lunch-time when he got back to the Marquis of Tenterton and Honeybody already had his napkin tucked in the top of his waistcoat and a pint of bitter beside him.

"What was the verdict?" he asked sourly.

"Open," said Honeybody. "A wonderful Crowner is old Mr. Tuit, no mucking about. Get it over quick, no awkward questions, and get the corpse under without delay. I met the grave-digger and he's having a field day, paid by the job as he is. He says Dr. Tulkingham is rare snaky as *he* doesn't get paid by the job, though the undertaker usually slips him a little. And at three o'clock he takes Miss Sloper and the Coroner's officer thinks you should come along as a solicitor is down from London to watch the family interests. Nothing to it—'murder by a person unknown'."

"Many from the press?" asked Harry as he ordered.

"The County papers only, headed by the *Granchester Week Gazette*, but they are starting to arrive."

Pretending to study the wine list, the Chief Inspector looked around. He recognised six familiar faces, with one stout, blue-rinsed lady of formidable aspect trying to catch his eye as she sipped her double gin between mouthfuls of mixed grill.

"Can't you go?" he whined. "After all . . ."

"They might crucify you if you didn't, sir.' When he called Harry 'sir' Sergeant Honeybody was being very serious. "If you go it's all right because I came to an understanding with the Coroner's officer and old Mr. Tuit does what he says."

A purblind, senile solicitor, Mr. Tuit, pronounced *Tweet*, was known to Harry by repute as England's most inept coroner, which was saying something. In the profession he was known as 'a major coronary disaster'. He groaned and ate his omelette without appetite while Honeybody wisely shut up.

Mr. Tuit got himself well bogged down on the medical evidence and kept enquiring the cause of death.

"The bullet entered her brain through an aperture between her eyes," the pathologist had said.

"An aperture between her eyes," said old Mr. Tuit doubtfully surveying the six jurymen seated on the hard seats of Dr. Tulkingham's Parish Hall. Two quid the Vicar pocketed per case, Honeybody, red faced and lurking at the back of the crowded hall, had said.

"A bullet hole," snarled the pathologist.

"Can I see the bullet?"

"That is not my business, sir. It was obviously fired from a high-velocity rifle, and had in fact become merely a pellet of metal when I, um, recovered it."

Old Mr. Tuit surveyed his fob watch and called upon Harry. "Did you see the bullet, Chief Inspector?" he asked after the swearing-in.

"No, sir, she went to the window. She dropped dead. I saw a star in the window."

"A star, was it dark? I remember it was a very fine night."

"A star-shaped hole in the glass, caused I presume by a bullet."

"Ah!" exclaimed Mr. Tuit. "Such as might have made the hole in her head."

"Precisely, sir."

It seemed touch and go whether Mr. Tuit, chin low, would actually go to sleep, but the London solicitor, moustache bristling, was on his unsteady feet. "I take it that Miss Sloper, deceased, was mercilessly shot whilst under police protection."

"I do not know about mercilessly," said Harry, "but she had never asked for any protection. She had asked me and my Sergeant home for a convivial drink. It was, in a sense, a social occasion."

"But you were on duty?"

"Not at that hour in the sense you mean. She was a respected local resident: some of my business, the apparent suicide of a man named Title, might have been discussed over a friendly glass."

"There is no suggestion, surely, that the deceased lady was mixed up in anything of an illegal nature?"

"Good Lord, no. We make it a practice to have a gossip to reputable citizens to get the atmosphere of a village. Miss Sloper was noted for her good works."

Fifteen guineas, thought the solicitor, had been earned, and sat down.

Mr. Tuit roused himself and summed up. Violence was rife, old standards should become more attractive to the young, rifles should be banned entirely, no doubt a drunken prank terminated the life of an estimable lady, but it was his duty to advise that 'murder by a person unknown' was the proper verdict.

"Shouldn't it be 'persons'?" enquired a dismal juryman.

"Only one person can fire a rifle," declaimed Mr. Tuit with the air of Confucius.

Altogether it hadn't been too bad, mused Harry, except for old Mr. Tuit and his stupidity: with a sharper coroner it might have been unpleasant. In an effort to dodge the reporters he found himself in the ladies' loo where the stout old undertaker was screwing down the coffin, an ornate affair with chrome handles, but as the undertaker explained after offering a pull from his hip flask, the late lamented had been head of the local Girl Guides and he understood there was plenty of money. "Not what I usually get, the cheap eighty-quid cremation jobs and God knows what whining from friends and relatives when they realise that *I* don't supply the drink, though I used to have an arrangement with poor Mr. Lane to do the Wake, with a mere five per cent comish for yours truly. She goes to her Reward tomorrow morning, Dr. Tulkingham wanted several with one hit, so to speak. Mr. Title is having a good one, him being intestate and in no position to quarrel—not that the Irish stint on funerals, killing each other regular as they do: then there are two paupers from the Institution, just bread and butter as you might say..."

Harry escaped and took the bus to Granchester with the intention of going to the pictures. Experience had taught him that this was the most effective method of going to earth. Yet it was not to be. He got off at the Corn Exchange, feeling creaky, and a whiff of unpleasant breath came over his shoulder.

It was the man known as Dirty Douglas. Harry had no doubt he was getting his reward on earth, what with the Welfare State, Supplementary Benefit, pinching from parked cars and the dubious earnings—according to Honeybody—of his three elder daughters who had the kind of development which attracted American tourists. Douglas's clothes were, however, of a second-hand kind, with a light brown jacket over which somebody had been sick in the remote past and a bow tie with fresh tomato sauce smeared on it. He was carrying something wrapped in an old copy of the *News of the World*.

"P'raps we could 'ave a liddle natter, Mr. James, sir," offered Dirty Douglas furtively.

"Here and now?"

"Parm me, sir, but I've got me good name to consider. If it got about I was goin' up to policemen..."

"How the hell did you find me?"

"I was at the inquest, sir. I never miss 'em. Better than the telly and wiv no cost. I'm the Coroner's most faithful fan, sir, and his officer sometimes lets me view the body. We had a rare case last year, three heads coming off completely when the bus went over the Embankment. A rare sight, as the Coroner's officer, 'oo 'as a rare sense of fun, 'ad set them up separate on top of the cisterns in the ladies' loo. To get back to our liddle bit of business, I followed you into the bus, like, you looking a bit dopey and not seeing me."

"Get to the point."

Dirty Douglas polished one filthy shoe on the calf of the other leg. "Round the corner is a snug liddle place called the *Dragon*, sir, where I'm known. It's dry and a man could do with a generous gargle."

In fact the *Dragon* was an anachronism, a good old beer house presided over by a stout married couple who did not appear to wash much. The beer was unexpectedly good, and the portion of welsh rarebit—Harry was feeling a little faint—tasted superb, though produced from a sinister-looking iron contrivance.

"I was in the War, sir," said Dirty Douglas, unpleasantly huddled against the Chief Inspector in the darkest corner of the bar.

"I'm sure you did your duty."

"Three affiliation orders, sir, and a dishonourable discharge for flogging tea," leered Douglas, affably. "But I know how to take a gun apart, so when I found a bit of one this morning, I said to myself, 'Douglas, it's your dooty to see that nice friendly policeman.' Look!" He unravelled the *News of the World* until, reposing on an old story about a manufacturer of bathing dresses, was revealed an outsize stock of a fire-arm. Harry peered at it, recalling his forensic refresher courses. 'Hammerli' was stamped upon it, a target automatic from Switzerland, and probably the best of its kind, firing a lead bullet which would kill a lion at five yards. Known as LR or Long Rifle, it weighed a bit over two pounds and was eighteen inches long, but was the real pro job for assassination. It fired standard small-bore ammunition which made it anonymous. 'Good stopping power' was the technical jargon for its prowess, with a heavy fast bullet which spread on impact, unlike the cupro-nickle or zinc ones.

You had to have pretty strong hands to use the weapon unless it was affixed to a bench. No cartridge case had been found, in spite of the labours of umpteen policemen crawling on hands and knees, which pointed to the use of a loose fitting-bag over the slide—normally the ejected cartridge case would fly several yards to the right and no sensible murderer would tarry in the dark to recover it. However, it was not a woman's weapon, which at any rate ruled out Miss Stinting, but left Chef Beedle. He had been wearing a duffle coat, remembered Harry. You could conceal an A & R under a bulky coat.

"Where did you come across this object?" he asked.

Dirty Douglas progressed several notches up the slyness meter. "I've kind of forgotten, God bless me, what with getting older and more and more cares descending on me shoulders."

"How much?"

"Nothing at all, sir," said Dirty Douglas. "I know my dooty—eff me if the Captain and the bleedin' old padre wasn't on to us night, mornin' and day about it. But I 'ave a wife and a brood of children eating away from dawn to dusk . . ."

"Twenty quid," said Harry, getting out his wallet, "and if anybody ever asks you, you deny it."

The pound notes disappeared into some recess in Dirty Douglas's greasy coat. "When you come out of Sir Hugh's Estate, sir, the road leads along past the duckpond and the

Vicarage. Old Joe keeps the rain channel free on the duckpond side and is an old friend o' mine. This morning he was clearing the muck out of it, about nine it were, 'cause I got out early with seven females in the 'ouse, and he says 'Wot's this?' I told him it might come in useful to me and wrapped it up in this old paper that was flapping around in the breeze."

"Nothing else?"

Douglas shook his head reluctantly. "I don't reckon so. Old Joe does a thorough job at mucking-out and I hung around for the two hours it took him."

The Chief Inspector stood him another pint before leaving. He went to the office of the local Superintendent, who was remorselessly drinking weak tea and peering at reports.

"I've never seen one of those jobs," he grunted, peering at the stock. He got on to the telephone for a while. "Forensic reports that it could well be," he said at the end of his conversation. "The bullet was so splayed and flat that it gives us nothing. I presume there will be no fingerprints..."

"Not after the ditch and Dirty Douglas's handling, Super."

"It doesn't seem to have been in the ditch long," said the Superintendent. "Down here in the country you get a bit experienced about ditches and the things that get put into them. Last night or early this morning, I'd say. We are generally early birds hereabouts, those of us who have to earn a living."

"Who went out of the Palabras Estate this morning?"

From his crowded desk, the Super fished out a file. "Only this fellow Beedle," he said, "but it's according to pattern. He gets up at six, looks in to see that the old gent is still breathing, then pads off for a two-mile walk."

"Do you know his record?"

"You fellows sent down extracts from the files. Why we

allow Marxist wogs to come here is more than a senile old chap due for his pension can imagine. Why we ever allowed Marx here is equally strange to me." He popped his teeth. "Why should Beedle have killed Miss Sloper?"

"The documents that Palabras has or had."

"Curse all politicians. I personally searched the Abajo dwelling and there were no gun parts there, nor were there papers of the description we had."

"I suppose we had better have the ditches and drains searched. There is an eighteen-inch barrel hanging around, just long enough to be difficult to dispose of."

"We'll scavenge," agreed the Super, "and sometimes I think I should have gone into garbage collecting as a youngster. God knows the perks are more and the pension much the same."

"This Beedle had better be watched."

"I've got seven men round the Estate. With the terrain we cannot keep closer than that."

Chapter Six

Harry had dined on fish and chips in a gloomy Granchester emporium and scuttled into the Marquis of Tenterton in a successful effort to avoid Sergeant Honeybody, whose face he nevertheless encountered at breakfast. A red-looking face it was, intaking kipper.

"A lovely little inquest," said Honeybody. "You can't beat these senile old English crowners. They tell me the American ones are mostly sharp undertakers by profession who won't overlook nothing, being close up to the cadaver so to speak."

"What did old Tuit overlook?"

"There wasn't a sound of a shot."

"They don't make silencers for that type of gun," said Harry. "On the other hand they do not make too much noise, which only adds up to the fact that the killer was good enough to fire from near maximum range. The stock of an A & R was found in the ditch leading to the duckpond."

"A pro job," said Honeybody, removing a kipper bone from his front dentures, "that is if it is not a plant. I dare say you can pick up junked bits of weapons."

"It's a thought." The Chief Inspector drank the remains of his coffee. "The only thing is that there are not too many of these guns legitimately around, though there is a black market via Italy."

"A lot of Irish boys in Granchester," said Honeybody, his teacup refilled. "I spotted a couple of 'knowns' when the Coroner's officer was showing me the sights of the town. Fourteen fish-and-chips, a fourteenth-century whore-house now the site of the Salvation Army Citadel, an old Englishe tea shoppe, and a betting shop run by an old acquaintance, one Cheerful Charlie."

"He was the chucker-out in night clubs? That one?"

"Part-time poncing as well, but he thought bookmaking was more honest. He's got a head for figures." The Sergeant cackled. "He told me about the Irish boys, they wanting to have a bet on something at Bogside. Travelling in air-conditioning is their story. Charlie recognised 'em, as he never cared to chuck them out because of their habit of carrying gelignite in their rear pockets."

"They could be down for Justin Title's funeral."

"Are you going?"

"No."

"It would show respect to him and Miss Sloper, and besides, it might be interesting to watch faces. A lot of killers have been caught that way."

"All right," said Harry irritably.

"Dr. Tulkingham will start putting them down at the stroke of ten, providing the weather keeps fine as he suffers from his chest. I shall be occupied at Mr. Lane's inquest, the Coroner having asked me to identify."

"Are his next of kin over?"

"No," said Honeybody. "There wasn't much love lost, apparently. I had the occasion, with the Coroner's officer, to take a convivial glass with the solicitor's clerk who dealt with his affairs. After his third gin he said it wouldn't be a secret long. Lane's Estate is around twelve thousand pounds: he lived pretty well and played the ponies, otherwise it might have been more as he was on a percentage of the profits. Guess who he left it to?"

"For God's sake!" said the Chief Inspector.

"To Sir Hugh Palabras, 'his employer and a rare gentleman' as the will says!"

"When you've got it you get it," snarled Harry, thinking of his second mortgage.

"Nothing much to Palabras." Honeybody's small eyes twinkled as he rubbed salt into the wound. "Certainly it points to the fact that Lane worshipped Sir Hugh."

Harry remembered Hawker's words. "He has that effect on some people. He leaves me cold, but I suppose it is some question of a mental wave-length. Nevertheless Lane got the idea that Title was a threat to Palabras and poisoned him, little doubt of that. Poor devil. Title wasn't much chop however you look at him, a murderee if ever I investigated one. All right, I'll go to the funerals. Judging by Hawker's manner we'll be pulled off the case inside forty-eight hours."

Old Dr. Tulkingham, in his gloomy old church, the spire of which had long since fallen down, the debris having been used by a thrifty former incumbent for repairs to the Vicarage, did a combined service for Title, Miss Sloper and the two paupers who had fallen out of bed at the Institution. The church was fairly full, including the presence of Dirty Douglas, wearing tails. Obviously filched from the front seat of a parked Bentley, thought the Chief Inspector. "Those who have years to year, let them year," Dr. Tulkingham finally bayed, motioning to the genial old undertaker and his men. It was a carrying job, the enormous grave-yard—donated by an eccentric member of the Palabras family in 1810—being just outside the back entrance. Its chronically waterlogged condition from seepage from the duckpond caused the weeds to rise knee high so that one occasionally stubbed a toe or bashed a knee against a submerged tombstone. About fifty people preceded Harry in a kind of pecking order, led by the Vicar, who was flanked by the coffins, followed by Sir Hugh Palabras, General Edward Gould, Mrs. Peremely-Fox, the old woman who owned the tea shop, and somebody that Harry, from his furtive look, deduced was the local Councillor. They skirted the Palabras vault, built in green and orange marble on to the side of the church and free of weeds, and plashed through the verdant greenery.

"A nasty job diggin' down in all that water," the gravedigger and his mate were whining to the Vicar, their long blond hair flowing over their collars.

"Quaite! Quaite!" said Dr. Tulkingham.

"It should be double time so the Transport Union Shop Steward said."

"Transport!" said the Vicar.

"If this ain't bleedin' transportation, Christ knows wot is," said the mate.

"We will discuss it later with the Vestrymen," said Dr. Tulkingham, nervously scratching around his dog collar.

Falling behind, the gravedigger addressed himself bitterly to Harry. "He ain't got no vestrymen save schoolmaster. Six old women and the horganist is wot e's got, plus sixty quid a week from the endowments and wot he fiddles."

"Was Mr. Lane a Protestant?"

"I 'eard 'im say the whole lot was bloody rot."

"Now, Lou," said the assistant, "it's fifteen nicker each."

"If we didn't do it where'd he get an hexperienced digger? I'm going to get my girl to write to Mr. Feather about another twenty-five per cent. Schoolteachers are goin' to get it, but 'ooever heard of a schoolteacher making a decent 'ole?"

In this Christian atmosphere Title, Miss Sloper and the paupers were laid to rest. Harry noticed that on the slippery sides of the graves the Vicar was very nippy on his pins and wondered if he might be younger than he looked. Looking about he saw one very Irish face. He edged near.

"Interested in Protestant ritual, Paddy? Converted by the Rev. Paisley?"

"Bit small for a demon, aren't you?" The man was good humoured and towered over Harry.

"Brains baffle bull, but if I couldn't take you in myself I can get ten men here within so many minutes so don't get out the gelignite."

"No sweat, mate. You'd be Yard, I think. We're not looking for trouble, just curious about Justin Title."

"A rat, wasn't he?"

The man's smoky eyes narrowed. "So you know. Yeah, he was a rat, but one is born every minute. He was doin' a little work for my friends, and he wasn't the kind of man to suicide."

"Work about some papers?"

"If you know a lot why ask me?"

Harry shrugged, and watched Dr. Tulkingham darting agilely to Miss Sloper's remains, while the gravediggers shovelled earth over Title's coffin. In priority the paupers were to be last.

"Perhaps we might trade a little information," said the Irishman softly.

"I'll trade."

"No good hanging about here. I thought I might spot somebody, but it's a dead duck, though why is Palabras here? He's no friend of the Irish."

"One of the others was his tenant, a Miss Sloper."

"I read about it. My car's parked outside. We could talk a little in it."

They slipped out through the lych-gate. Harry had the unpleasant feeling that he was being watched.

The car was a nondescript Volvo, with fifty thousand miles on the clock. Mentally the Chief Inspector recorded its number. The Irishman grinned. "We hire the cars," he said, "from friends, and never use them more than the month. Cigarette?"

Harry declined.

"We had a lot against Title." The Irishman settled himself behind the wheel and wound down the window. "But somebody had the idea that a rat like him could be pressured, and make no bones about it he was a smooth and capable individual. And we didn't want a shootin' over here. Then we were tipped off about this file, a bomb that would bring down the Government and destroy public confidence to an astounding degree. It was delivered to Palabras and we awaited publication, but nothin's happened for months. We reckoned that a smart fellah like Palabras, God rot him, might have sold out, so we approached this supple character, Title, who had become a crook's agent. He could probably have made fifteen thousand out of the Italians or the French if he had got his dirty hands on it, and we would have let bygones."

"There's another name in it, a genuine suicide. The publican where Title stayed. His name was Lane, 'Bosky' Lane. An Irishman whose son was shot in the affair you obliquely mention."

"God moves in strange ways," the Irishman declared. "The boy's father, of all the publicans around!"

"Nothing proven," said Harry. "Suicide while unsound."

"And mortal sin, the poor devil."

"One supposes you might have been a trifle resentful if Title had betrayed your own son."

"That would be different—and you the polis! I've half a mind to report ya." He was a quarter serious.

"Palabras intends to publish to the best of our knowledge. He's buying a newspaper for the purpose. But the file is going up and down like a yo-yo."

"Is it with Palabras?"

"His house was searched. Nothing there."

A FILE ON DEATH

"A cunning devil like him would find a way," said the Irishman. "A fellah with no moral principles whatsoever, as God's my witness. But it eases my mind a bit to hear it said. I'll give you a little. The Africans want that document badly. We'd prefer not, a pack of niggers being of no use to the old country. Now I'd better be pushing away."

The Chief Inspector stood on the road as the Volvo rushed off.

Presently the mourners came past the church, their heads bowed in an embarrassed similitude of grief. In the rear rank there was the stalwart figure of Chef Beedle, his ebony skin making the black suit he wore assume a bluish tinge as the sunlight momentarily poured between the clouds.

The crowd broke up, some into cars, others consulting their watches with a view to seeing how far off was Opening Time. A largish lady, clad in black, with a proprietary air about her, was accompanied by a mouseyish, tall man who to Harry's trained eye resembled Miss Sloper. They started to walk briskly past the Vicarage in the general direction of the Palabras Estate. He caught up with: "I'm a police inspector, sir. Would you be related to Miss Sloper?"

"Ah, yah, yerse," said the tall man with a kind of bray. "John Sloper, and, ah, yah, this is Mrs. Sloper. We've come from Town, ah, yah, for the funeral. I'm deceased's first cousin and her heir. We thought we'd go and view the, ah, yah, property."

"We explained all this to the police officer who visited us in Hampstead last evening," said Mrs Sloper sensibly. "We could not come conveniently to the Inquest—pointless to anyway—because John lectures at the University."

"Ah, yah, yerse," agreed Mr. Sloper.

"Did you see her often? I mean we're clutching at straws!"

"She used to come to London once a fortnight," said Mrs.

Sloper, "and probably once a month we used to meet her at a small Soho restaurant."

"Yerse and we used to come to Christmas, ah, yah. Well, we must be getting along. I have a busy day tomorrow."

"Did she ever mention anything about a purloined file?"

"I told her about it, if, ah, yah, we are talking of the same thing. It had reached my, er, ears through an Indonesian friend. What one would expect in an ah, yah, inherently imperialist society." He resumed his footsteps, peering apprehensively sideways at Harry.

"It appears she might have been trying to retrieve the papers."

"Let me tell the Inspector," said Mrs. Sloper. "John's cousin used to work for Security, one of these incompetent agencies. You must know that."

"I know it all right."

"She had a grievance against them . . . something to do with her retirement. It appeared to her that if she could retrieve the documents, she could make certain people look very silly, as they are. She was, I may say, a middle-of-the-road Tory in her political thinking."

"Did she like Palabras?"

"She thought him dangerous."

"A neo-fascist, ah, yah," declared John Sloper. "Could be the ruin of the country . . . a lot of fellows who should know better support him."

"Good-day, er, good-day." John Sloper dragged his wife into a kind of shambling trot.

"Miss Sloper's heir!" It was Palabras, beautifully groomed, carrying a stick. "A parlour pink! Did he have anything to contribute?"

"He indicated that Miss Sloper was after a certain file."

"Hm. A meddlesome old bitch, one is bound to say. So

was her aunt from whom she inherited. Liked power, relished it for its own sake. Well, who killed her?"

"I like Chef Beedle."

"Abajo's coloured cook! I would have thought that poor old Abajo's rice concoctions were more in his line than firearms."

"He is a Marxist of sorts!"

"So are we all, including old Abajo who must have a quarter of a million pounds. I advise him a bit on his finances and he prefers the most hide-bound of old companies with bad labour records."

"When do you intend publishing the file?" Harry asked bluntly.

"Sweating, are they?" Palabras chuckled. "Well, they have made a lot of people sweat in their time. So long, Chief Inspector." He swung his stick at a dandelion as he walked off.

Before lunch, Harry telephoned the county forensic laboratory. "How long to dismantle an A & R?"

"The Sloper shooting? I'm looking at the stock now. In water for up to twenty hours: the firearm was probably seven years old, quite well worn in fact. These hot jobs get peddled from hand to hand. Dismantling depends on experience and circumstances: I would not like to risk misleading you. Most of the pros have a kind of holster attached to their shin. Simple to slip it down your trousers if you wear the fancy bell-bottom type."

Perhaps he should drop the thing, mused Harry. He should have taken Chef Beedle to the Station on the night of the shooting. It was hindsight, but there was nothing his elders and betters delighted in more than that commodity.

Honeybody was lunching the Coroner on expenses, a fat amiable old man who opined that a good claret was the healthiest beverage as the result of hearing many pathological reports.

"A great deal of sin in the Parish," said Mr. Tuit over an oyster. "I was talking to Dr. Tulkingham—as you may know he has a scientific bent—and he agrees. There are more enquiries about deaths in Waddington Parva than the rest of my Parishes put together. Of course, there is the Institution here, though heaven knows they are strapped into bed, but the straps break and then they fall out. We used to have Australian straps, which held 'em until the doctor could give a certificate, but now they have to be Belgian and donkey-hide, which does not restrain them. More work for me who am on a fixed stipend. I wonder why they say that claret does not go with oysters?"

"What about lower beds?" asked Harry.

"The Home Office prescribed height is six feet to facilitate liberal use of colonic irrigation," said Mr. Tuit, "the Home Office being a great believer in it and wet blankets for the senile. I must say, Sergeant, that one could hardly resist the duckling."

"Do you know a Chef Beedle?" asked Harry.

"A gentleman of colour?" eventually asked Mr. Tuit when his duck had been boned. "I know his master, old Mr. Abajo—one dares say one might have to do him one day as he is so tottery. A fine chef, but garlicky. I do not mind it, but the Honourable Mrs. Tuit has a repugnance to it. Of course the Queen's Coroners have to have strong noses."

"A political man?" asked Harry.

"A coloured chef political!" exclaimed Mr. Tuit.

"As a civil servant to another, in a manner of speaking," said Harry, "I wonder whether Beedle did shoot Miss Sloper."

Mr. Tuit was not the fastest thinker in the world and he

obviously liked his duck well chewed. It was a matter of some twenty minutes before he spoke again. "It's a curious thing," he said, blinking his pale, watery blue eyes, "but this man Beedle goes up to London quite a lot."

"What happens about the old gent?" exclaimed Honeybody. "He can't fend for himself."

"The Honourable Mrs. Tuit," said the Coroner who obviously relished his wife's rank, "can only obtain part-time help. One of her standbys is a sturdy woman whom she likes to have as often as is possible. Unfortunately, on these London expeditions, Beedle engages this woman as a locum on generous terms. He prepares food before he leaves so that it can be reheated. Sometimes twice a week, though he does not seem to have gone to London as yet this week."

"Strange," said Harry but the Coroner had lost interest in anything except the menu.

"Mr. Tuit was very anxious to meet you, Harry," said the Sergeant later. They were seated in the lounge over coffee. The old Coroner had hastened away on matters concerning a traffic accident.

"You mean you wangled it as an excuse for unlimited eating: did you see what that claret cost?"

"It doesn't grow on trees," said Honeybody slopping rum into coffee. "Besides, you got some information regarding Beedle."

"Quite by chance."

"Where do we go from here, sir?" soothed the Sergeant.

"Back to report defeat. No gun, no papers, a tenuous suspicion of a black chef."

"Pull him in!"

"He has a perfectly good French passport and he's black. The howls that would eventuate if I took him in on suspicion would be more than my uniform is worth. Only one thing, I'd like to take a look at the house. I know the local Super directed the search and I think he's a first-class technician, but you get these niggling feelings and prickings in the thumbs."

"Suppose we take it in turns watching when he leaves the house. He must make some arrangement for the door to be opened when he's taking time off."

"No time like the present," said Harry while Honeybody, looking forward to a second rum, clearly regretted putting up the idea.

Luck, however, was with them as only a quarter of an hour elapsed as they strolled, becomingly aimlessly, on the other side of the road to the entrance to the Palabras Estate, before Chef Beedle came hurrying in the direction of the bus stop.

"He seems to go into Granchester a lot," said Harry.

"The shops are pretty lousy in the village," said Honeybody. "The locals go to Granchester which is a bit better."

"Let's get going."

The shutters were half closed on Mr. Abajo's house, giving the false illusion of desertion commonly found in Spanish countries. The Chief Inspector hesitated, then pushed at the front door. It opened and they went in, only to be confronted by Miss Drinkwater.

"Didn't expect to find you here," said Harry.

"Beedle does not like leaving Señor Abajo alone, though he sleeps most of the time. It's easy for me to slip over for the odd hour while he shops in Granchester. There's a little workroom with a typewriter."

"We're looking for the gun which killed Miss Sloper," said Harry bluntly. "I do not think it necessary to rouse the old gentleman. I suppose that you, as temporary custodian, have no objection?"

"My, how formal!" mocked Miss Drinkwater. "As long as you don't awaken Abajo, search away."

"A chef," said Honeybody licking his lips in an associational way, "thinks in terms of kitchens."

A FILE ON DEATH

"I think a rifle would rather stick out in a kitchen," said Miss Drinkwater doubtfully. Nevertheless the three of them went into the large, tiled, spotless room. Honeybody peered into cupboards, sniffing at the smells. "Every known herb or spice," he commented, "a small fortune in the most expensive Indian rice and such things as hot peppers, dried capsicums and real saffron. But no gun."

Harry had peered into the large refrigerator, which held little except milk and dried Spanish ham.

"The deep freeze is a very large one," commented Miss Drinkwater, looking at the white, horizontal cabinet in the corner.

It contained only a small, pink, deeply frozen piglet and a few packets of sweet corn. "Chef Beedle doesn't care for frozen food," said Miss Drinkwater, "accustomed as he was in his backward country to buy fresh provender in small quantities in the local markets."

Suddenly a bell rang for Harry. He took the pig out.

"The Spanish love suckling pig, which is hardish to come by," said Miss Drinkwater in her rather schoolmarmish manner. "It is depicted in one of their carvings of the Last Supper, which seems improbable."

The Chief Inspector took down one of Beedle's gleaming array of knives and slit down the pig, his left hand stinging from the cold. The knife had a serrated edge, and he sawed away.

"I say," Honeybody expostulated.

"We're not eating the bloody thing, and I suppose it will be cut up anyway. Look!" The knife grated against the rear sight of a gun barrel.

"Beedle!" said Miss Drinkwater. "I can make a few quid out of this—'in a pig's eye' or words to that effect."

"Can't stop you, love," said Harry as they sat down to wait for the Chef's return.

Chapter Seven

THE ROOM WAS cold and uncomfortable, as many interrogation rooms are. The lighting was very bright, because although one cannot lay a hand on a suspect, beyond perhaps painfully tripping violent men up, there is nothing in Judges' Rules to say you have to make them feel at home. Chef Beedle sat, slightly shivering, on a small kitchen chair, his buttocks drooping over on either side.

The local Super had not been very pleased. "Of course I didn't look up the bloody pig's arse," he had snarled when the news hit him. "I leave peering up arses to you London lot." He had been inclined to expatiate on the point until the sudden arrival of his superior officer, a bland man who liked harmony, or so he often said when in any difficulty.

The Super, Harry and Honeybody were surveying Beedle from their upholstered chairs. It was ten o'clock at night and so far the Chef had been taciturn, expressing only alarm for the well-being of Señor Abajo to whom a District Nurse had been dispatched.

"Now, Mr. Beedle," said Harry, "you must realise that if you cannot give some reasonable explanation we might have to charge you."

"With what?"

"The firing chamber and a barrel of a rifle were inside that pig. You have, by your own admission, no licence to possess a firearm of any description."

"I want my consul and my solicitor."

"A consular representative will arrive here at nine o'clock tomorrow morning. Your solicitor is visiting North Africa. I have offered to get you a local one."

"I don't want a white solicitor."

"Perhaps any solicitor, black, white or green, might be hard pressed to explain how parts of a gun were in a deep freeze under your control. I suppose you do not suggest that Señor Abajo goes in for gunnery."

"*I* suppose that you planted it there."

"There was an independent witness, Miss Drinkwater."

Chef Beedle looked taken aback. "She is a nice kind lady who is not racist. I would believe her. But somebody must have come in and planted it. If Señor Abajo is asleep, I occasionally go out, a man cannot stay around the house all the time. I leave the front door unlocked." He shrugged. "It is the lesser of two evils. If there was a fire, I would not wish the old gent to be locked in, you know. I don't broadcast the fact, but somebody might know."

"You go to London a lot," said Harry.

"Then, man, I arrange for a highly respectable lady to come in to look after the Master. I leave him his delicacies and have instructed her how to reheat them."

"Makes a bit of a hole out of your wages," said the Super, popping his teeth.

"That is my business." The Chef achieved a certain dignity.

"Politics is your business, I think," said Harry.

"Anti-imperialism is my business," said Beedle, "whether Russian, Yankee, French, British, or Chinese. What law is against that?"

"None," said the Super, washing his hands of that line of talk.

"Look here, Chef Beedle," Honeybody was at his most

avuncular, fairly sweating friendship. "Let's not muck about. A bit of a chat and we can all have a kip. Some grub sent in for you and a nice bottle of wine on the house. Whatever you say can't be used in evidence—you have not been warned. Why not a little chat and off to bed? There's a matter of some stolen file in the background."

"I did not kill Miss Sloper."

"In the end, old chap, that will be a matter for gents in wigs and everybody lying their heads off. We can probably prove you were after the stolen file—in your business there is always a grass."

"I was interested in a file, a disgraceful file about a disgraceful business. I only wished to see it published, that men's hearts should be opened to realise the iniquities of their rulers."

"And Miss Sloper was an obstacle?" asked Honeybody smoothly.

"I wish to see a solicitor," said Beedle, "a white solicitor if there is no alternative."

"Too late tonight," said the Super, "but if you wouldn't mind our most comfortable cell, the one with a proper loo in it, plus fish and chips and a bottle, we'll get you one by nine thirty or ten tomorrow, the Granchester lawyers not being given to early rising."

"I want my rights."

The Super suddenly looked older. "I suppose Miss Sloper had some rights." Chef Beedle looked at him puzzled. The Super pressed a button, two uniformed men came through the door and led Chef Beedle away.

Harry went over and lit the gas fire.

"The case is full of holes," he said.

"He was near the crime, had a motive, and bits of the gun were in the deep freeze," said the Super. "I think it is up to the Director of Public Prosecutions." He eyed Harry shrewdly. "I dare say you will do the report."

"I expect so, sir," said Harry dutifully.

Honeybody sat on the end of Harry's bed as the Chief Inspector finished phoning Inspector Hawker.

"God knows what the press will do about this pig," was his superior's first, groaned comment. "Then there's the Bacon Producers' Council, which carries a lot of weight. Why the hell couldn't he have used New Zealand lamb?"

"I'll dictate a report for the Director," said Harry "suggesting that Beedle be detained on the minor charge of concealing weapons." He could envisage Hawker, in the private bedroom he had at the Yard, seated at the side of his bed wearing the red flannel nightshirt that he wore winter and summer to protect his kidneys.

Switched over to the recording department, Harry gave the usual report for the solicitors and hung up.

"I wish we had never got into this," grumbled Honeybody. "No prints on the barrel, the door kept unlocked, everybody claiming that Beedle is an innocent, black patriot with the highest motives. I just suppose that old Spaniard could not have done it. They are a revengeful lot—I remember a melon salesman in Covent Garden who poured boiling oil over his girl friend."

"Abajo is over 90, I checked him with *Who's Who*. At that age you don't fire rifles. No, it must be Beedle. I wonder if he had contacts in Granchester."

"Some of the fruit shops and fish-and-chippers are owned by Afros, and there is a Mao restaurant, specialising in health foods, run by an Indian."

"I suppose we'll sweat in tomorrow. First thing, you go

and seek Dirty Douglas—he seems to be literally a depository of all the dirt. If anybody knows anything about Beedle, or anybody come to that, it would be this stinking man."

"He fairly does get about, by report," said Honeybody, "listening at windows, robbing telephone boxes, a bit of petty blackmail no doubt—cunning as a lavatory rat, as the Aussies say."

Chef Beedle had passed a good night. "Apart from complaining about the egg and chips plus tinned plums and condensed milk which were provided for him on instructions," grumbled the local Sergeant, "refusing the baked beans and a bottle of British burgundy, he's like an old black lamb. I don't like it, sir. They generally fuss and fret upon felony sush. He's calm and collected. A Frenchman came down from the London Consulate, smelling like a hair-oil factory, and is with him now. Old Mr. Crabble, the solicitor, is waiting to see him."

The local Super, out early and a little before Harry, and bad tempered about it, said "We'd better see old Crabble. His family has been persecuting widows and orphans for roughly three hundred years in this part of the country. Very sly, very knowing."

Crabble proved on the timeless side, his silvered blond hair above a ruddy complexion belying his years, which might have been in the middle seventies.

"Mr. Beedle has a French consular official with him," said the Super after introductions were over.

"Ah!" Mr. Crabble's look reflected his youthful trips to Calais. "Hm! Is there a sexual angle?"

"No," said the Super.

"To be frank a British jury will think a Frenchman

capable of anything, which is why the Government could not go to the country on the Common Market. When you telephoned me, and I confess I had drunk my hot milk and retired, you said that part of a gun had been found inside a deep-frozen pig."

"A pig substantially in the custody of your client."

Mr. Crabble had a set of false teeth which rivalled the Super's. After whistling through them rather pleasantly—*The Skaters' Waltz* Harry thought—he said, "My grandfather, in 1857, defended an excise case involving a dozen bottles of prime port in a dead mule. Case dismissed, on the ground that the mule was the custodian of the contraband. On that precedent the pig was custodian of the rifle."

"The mule was not deep frozen!"

"That is to be proven: it might have been a hard winter."

"A pig is hardly likely to have fired a bullet."

"Is that the charge, firing rather than mere possession?"

"The charge would be possession of an unregistered firearm," said the Super.

"Suppose he went to Granchester for the morning Session, pleaded not guilty, and was released on moderate bail," said the solicitor.

The Super remained silent, looking at Harry, who said, "We would agree, preferring him, as an alien, to surrender his passport."

"That is for the Magistrates," declared Mr. Crabble, but with a friendly air.

"All right," said Harry. "We had better go and see him."

By courtesy of the official electric razor and dabblings in the cramped bathroom, Chef Beedle looked fairly well-groomed. He was seated opposite a youngish Frenchman, who, contrary to the Sergeant's prejudices, smelled only of bacon and eggs. But he was voluble. Chef Beedle had the right to return to France where justice was Napoleonic, de Gaullist and logical. There were precedents—the Red Max case for instance.

"*Merde*," said the Super, surprisingly.

"I dare say that at this delicate political moment, one would not wish to make an issue," said the Frenchman.

"Take your issues to Whitehall," said the Super, "where some of them speak schoolboy French, or so I'm told. I retire in two months and now nobody can take away my little bit of pension."

"I understand," the consular official smiled. "There is no quarrel, but Mr. Beedle should be released from custody."

"I am his solicitor," said Mr. Crabble, "and fortunately we are not governed by Roman Law under which Mr. Beedle could be held indefinitely, so it is a case of bail, if granted! The charge concerns firearms in a pig. Under the custody of Mr. Beedle!"

"*Charcuterie*," said the Frenchman, alarmed at his weakest point. "It is barbarous to place firearms in a pig. Saltpetre is known, but metal!"

"Rice, raisins, pine nuts, a trifle of cinnamon, oil and some people like nutmeg," said Chef Beedle, with dismal authority. "The pig was deep frozen, which I regret, but the insertion of firearms was unknown to me."

"A Spanish recipe!" said the Frenchman.

"It's all right," said Beedle, taking umbrage.

"A *confit* of the liver?" suggested the Frenchman.

"Not with many herbs," said Beedle. "The French tend to over season pork."

"That is a matter of opinion!"

"Now, gents," said Mr. Crabble, "just a not-guilty plea on possession of firearms, no mention of the pig, and bail in Granchester." He cocked a disapproving English eye in the direction of the Frenchman. "And no *ad hoc* referenda about whether your countrymen approve!"

"We should discuss this as civilised persons," said the consular representative.

"Now, monsewer," said the Super, "the English have a coarse sense of 'umour. Pigs are funny. Rifles in pigs are funnier. We don't want to put on a nigger-minstrel show." He caught sight of Chef Beedle and blushed violently.

"I don't mind the term," said Beedle, softly, "in practical terms I do not want to be involved in a knockabout comedy concerned with pigs. The nigger minstrels, I believe, were generally Jewish anyway."

"Well," said the Super, "you have to make the decision. But I do not mind simply laying the charge of concealed weapons before the Bench and not opposing bail. I suppose it would be a matter of a hundred pounds."

"That would be no trouble," said Beedle.

"A man of wealth?" asked the Super.

"One has friends."

"I wish coppers did. Righto! We'll get into Granchester by ten."

Harry was grateful for the comfort of the official Humber. What had once been a moot-hall in the year 1300 was the old Granchester Petty Sessions where a certain Captain Cockworthy (Rtd.) presided over two elderly and depressed fellow magistrates, and a suety-faced clerk who in fact did the work. It had the odd smell which accretes around police courts. Cockworthy's hearing aid was of mercurial disposition and proceedings were conducted either in yells or in whisperings. Outside pigs screamed as they were hauled into trucks.

"A French citizen, and a concealed weapon," said Cockworthy, who was right on the ball. "Politics involved?"

"We have no reason to suppose so," said the local Super. "No objection to bail, Yer Honour."

"We may not relish the idea of having foreigners running around with lethal weapons," said Cockworthy, bending towards the Clerk who talked into the hearing aid with authority.

"Bail at one hundred pounds and surrender of passport,'" said the Chairman at length and Harry slipped away. Granchester at eleven is curiously lacking in life. Trucks rumble from the brewery, noises—snatches of obscene, time-honoured rhymes—are chanted by pupils in the ancient primary school. There is a smell of cow manure, rotten fruit and beer, but it is a good place for the nerves and Harry felt relaxed as he glanced down the main street, fortunately by-passed, towards the old toll-gate. He knew that the pubs were opening, and it was merely a matter of time before Honeybody approached the largest, the old Duke of Edinburgh, named after Queen Victoria's son on his return from Australia a hundred years ago. Sure enough, the Sergeant lumbered into sight, as placid as a roast of beef and as English. He was scratching his buttocks in meditation.

"Honeybody," yelled Harry from across the street.

"Time for a bit of lubrication, guv'nor," said the good Sergeant when they met up. "No good getting dry in this game whatever the ladies may say! A pint and a meat pie as a tightener would be most welcome, and, dear me, their mutton pies are famous, with a blandness about them."

Inside Harry chose orange juice, but weakened in favour of a small shot of vodka.

"I saw Dirty Douglas," said the Sergeant through his fourth mouthful of pie. "Two quid and a cup of coffee in a dirty pull-up on the town's edge. Very ripe: we should get danger money like the dockers. 'They'—you know 'they', the petty crooks Douglas associates with—are curious about Beedle. Douglas tried to sell him a nice widow but he recoiled: so they tried him with boys, an illustrated *Kama Sutra,* a smuggled Jap transistor which will get anywhere, a stolen electric shaver and a hot motor bike. No go! They reckon that a bloke who turns down all of that is a crook. When he comes in here he sees the Indian, Chandy, who runs the Mao Restaurant, specialising in 'food for the brain' whatever that might be."

"Sesame seed," sighed Harry, who had done a tour of health shops.

"Chandy is married," said the Sergeant, absent-mindedly ordering himself an ale. "Five children and keeps to himself as the Indians tend. He started five months ago: rice muck with some kind of spiel about it. Customers are the bearded ones, but not enough to support the place."

"When you have finished drinking," said Harry unpleasantly, "we will see Chandy and try to gaff him. I never knew an Indian you could bully, but we'll see."

The Mao Restaurant was not big, but Mr. Chandy was, exuding a kind of benignness which made right-thinking men long to attack him with a blunt instrument.

"Chef Beedle," he said smoothly, "is anti-imperialist. He is a friend."

"All I know about successive imperialisms is that they tended to introduce running water and crappers," said Harry.

"Oh, very good, very to the point. But surely there could be anti-imperialist crappers? We will not quarrel on that point."

"A file of papers?" asked Harry. "Do you know about them?"

"Hoist with your own petard, my dear fellow," said Mr. Chandy. "Neither Beedle nor I wrote that file, but being written it is dynamite."

"You are 'in' with Beedle?"

Mr. Chandy had big white teeth. "I dare say Beedle and

I may think alike. We would prefer the papers to be published, perhaps in Africa rather than Europe. Why should the devil have all the good songs, as you asked in England a hundred years ago?"

"Miss Sloper was shot: the gun was inside Beedle's deep freeze."

Chandy looked at his hands, seriously. "It would not be in character with Beedle to shoot Miss Sloper, I think. She was a serious person, God knows, and many an orphan must be grateful to her, though that class of person *likes* orphans: a do-gooder."

"Perhaps a friend of Beedle's did it!"

Chandy's eyes momentarily flickered. "Not I, sir, I assure you, having a perfect alibi for the evening in question. It might be that Beedle knew violent men, fanatics who believe violence to be an argument. He is very far to the left, is Beedle, but of course his father was executed by the French, and his brother rather gruesomely killed by the current native rulers."

"One hardly associates a good chef with violence," mused Harry.

"You have never spent time in a professional kitchen, sir. The language is profane and violent. In my place, of course, we serve the food of peace, meditation and tranquillity. I would be pleased to have you as my guest."

Harry restrained an outward shudder and departed. He had not liked the expertise of Mr. Chandy and wondered who subsidised him.

Honeybody, who had kept silent, said, "A bull artist that one, all talk and no performance."

"He would be a 'drop'," replied the Chief Inspector. "He'd transmit orders and convey reports, perhaps pay Beedle his expense money."

"The left-wing boys want those papers to be published at any cost, eh?" said the Sergeant.

"And some right-wing boys. We'd better see the rest of the tradesmen."

Those Granchester shops which had survived the onslaught of several supermarkets lacked customers, except for the chain stores. They included a musty little place which dealt in underwear apparently designed for foxhunting squires in 1900. Honeybody, who favoured stout underwear, was fascinated and bought an undergarment reinforced with webbing and straps. The old gentleman who was behind the counter was overcome at this pick-up in sales, and was anxious to please as he laboured surreptitiously to remove the worst of the fly specks. However, he had never seen Beedle and they left him muttering that Mr. Powell was right. A herb and exotic fruit shop knew Beedle well, but the proprietor, a Nigerian, said his knowledge was purely on a business plane. "Apparently he works for a fellow whose taste buds have got to be tickled. I used to order Indonesian condiments for him—I can get you anything. He knew a great deal about cooking, I think."

"A bit left in his views, wasn't he?" said Honeybody, innocently.

"He never talked politics," said the proprietor, "though he told me where he came from and I guessed he was out of sympathy with the regime."

For the rest, it was either "Can't remember him," or "Oh, yes, a black cook, isn't he? Buys the best quality but small quantities."

It started to rain hard and a wind sprang up. Harry was very tired when at seven o'clock they got to the Marquis of Tenterton.

"Come up to my room," said Harry. "I'll get on to Hawker and report. We might as well go back tomorrow. I'll have a sandwich here and get to bed. It seems a week since I slept."

Before he could reach the handset there was a tap on the door.

"Come in!"

Mr. Quarles, who was deceptively fast on his feet, came in.

"Evening, Mr. James! This would be your good Sergeant, Mr. Honeybody. I'm Quarles, a battered old Whitehall Warrior."

Honeybody's face was blank as he shook hands.

Quarles took a seat on the bed.

"Suppose you give me a complete report, Chief Inspector."

"Very well. Hugh Palabras received a purloined file and kept it in an old, primitive safe. Justin Title, in bad odour with the I.R.A., was told to have it pinched, when bygones would be bygones. Miss Sloper spotted him for what he was and offered to pay him for delivery of the file. Her motive was to make Whitehall look silly. She was using her own money but presumably you would have had no alternative other than to reimburse her. Somebody, presumably Beedle, learned of this danger—an unsavoury character in the village had overheard their conversation—and shot her to prevent this. Palabras had meantime given the file for safe-keeping to the manager of this pub. His son had been betrayed by Title."

"Hardly betrayed," smirked Mr. Quarles. "Perhaps Title was obeying moral inclinations. The son and associates were plotting to blow up a crowded cinema where a Beatles film was being run, with two hundred pounds of dynamite activated by an inaccurate Irish-made alarm clock. I refreshed myself from the records. We paid Title seven hundred pounds and gave him free conduct and no prosecution for a few things the police had against him in London."

"Horrid but efficient little beast," said Harry, but not

aloud. Honeybody seemed fascinated by something on the ceiling.

"I think he sensed that Title was plotting something against Palabras and this was the last straw. He planted the odds and ends of barbiturates left behind by guests in Title's private brandy bottle. Eventually it preyed on Lane's conscience to the extent that he took his life. I think we would find his manner had been a little strange since Title's death."

"One of the barmaids, sir, did tell me that instead of the usual Jolly-Jack performance, he was snappy and morose the days before he died, but I thought it was a woman's imagination." Honeybody was unctuous.

"And the file?" asked Quarles.

"We found the cover, that is all. I think the point was that the thick cardboard was unwieldy to bend, which means that the contents were folded and then parcelled or enveloped. Before going to bed Lane delivered them somewhere, probably by hand . . ."

"I do not think that he saw Palabras personally," said Quarles, "my information coming from Miss Stinting. Apart from the fact that a man contemplating suicide does not want to meet people . . . It is a solitary business. Miss Stinting tells me that there is a large letterbox on the porch of the Palabras house, steel-reinforced and unlocked by a key which Sir Hugh keeps on his personal key-ring. I imagine Lane walked there, put the envelope in, and came back home. By the way, I'm booked in here. I saw you arrive from my window."

"One imagines you have a better room than I."

"The place emptied today. The press stories of sudden death frightened people away. Now then, you and I, Mr. James, will go and see Palabras. The Sergeant can hold the fort here. Sir Hugh has a dinner for six guests, important ones. It puts a man on the wrong foot when an inspector calls in such circumstances."

"Will he see you? He mentioned you and I gathered..."

"That he disliked me!" Quarles gave an impersonal hangman's smile. "That is very true, but he'll see me because he has an overriding curiosity. If he did not he'd not sleep for a week."

Harry got to his feet, conscious that tiredness and lack of food had made him feel slightly sick. "I'll get a sandwich at the bar," he said, "then we'll go."

A butler of morose mien had ushered them into Sir Hugh's workroom with some dubiousness after examining Harry's professional card. In five minutes the baronet appeared dressed for dinner, looking a trifle harassed.

"Oh, Quarles," he said, without his habitual smile.

"Yes, Hugh, we meet again, and none too soon. I always have hoped we could have lunch one day."

Palabras seated himself, started to say something but refrained.

"I've come for the file," said Quarles, simply. "As a favour to you, for old times' sake."

"Curse your impudence!"

"They were a plant, Hugh!"

Palabras's eyes narrowed. "Look here," he said, "I have guests entertaining each other. In precisely twenty-five minutes we sit down to dine."

"The forgeries were documented, sworn to be false on affidavit by those alleged to have written the documents, several months before we rather elaborately planted them on you. We are not fools! The man who did the stealing was never more than a step in front of the security agent, to the rage of my accounting officer. We thought from the background the file would end up with you. There was a chance that it would end up in a foreign Embassy, but we would not have minded, though for certain reasons we hoped it would be you."

"I do not believe it!"

"My dear Hugh, its publication would have made traditional Perfidious Albion look like a Salvation Army Officer. Our enemies would have crowed aloud, the French would have burned our Embassy out of sheer self-righteousness, Malta would have submitted a bill. Etcetera! Then we would have exploded *our* bomb, as soon as *Time* had finished serialising the stuff. A complete forgery, and a Cabinet minute, made over a year ago, to prove it! In the consternation that followed, we were, ahem, going to be a bit naughty and in effect steal somebody's clothes. It was the usual piece of misdirection with which you are familiar and at which all British Governments, bless them, are adept."

"But why come to me now?"

"The naughtiness we planned is no longer necessary. You read of the assassination yesterday? The C.I.A. accomplished it by direct methods. I must say our American friends go straight to the heart of the matter, in this case with a sawn-off shotgun," Mr. Quarles gave his liquid chuckle. "No, you see, Hugh, if you publish this in your new paper, we'll just raid, confiscate and seal the presses under an Emergency Order, then bring you up for uttering forged documents, the prosecution under orders to make you look a most ghastly old ass. On the other hand, if you play, I guarantee that for the first two issues you will be supplied with a few quite sensational stories for the front page."

Palabras was looking his age. He got up and walked to the window where he stood for a couple of minutes.

"I never know whether to believe you or not!" he said.

"Hugh!"

"Nevertheless you win. Here!" He came over to the desk, took his key-ring, apparently a permanent fixture, and opened a drawer. He brought out a bundle of papers. "I was going to take them up to London in the morning. Take them, man, they seem to have caused enough bloody trouble."

Quarles bowed his head, as one receiving a Communion wafer. On tiny feet he went over to the large, empty fireplace, placed the papers on the hob and applied a cigarette lighter to them. When they finished burning he stirred the ashes with a fire iron.

"There," he said, "I won't keep you from your dinner!"

A funny, mischievous smile came over Sir Hugh's face. "You aren't dressed," he said, "but we can always feed one more! Come and meet my guests."

"Delighted," said Quarles.

"I'd better get along," said Harry.

Sir Hugh gave him a cold, indifferent nod.

Looking wistfully at Quarles' Jag, at the side of an assortment of even more expensive hardware, Harry started the walk home. The paths felt very hard. He glimpsed Dr. Tulkingham manipulating a large net on the outskirts of a shrubbery, but luckily the Vicar did not see him, so intent was he upon his task of decimating the bird life. It was a relief to see Honeybody, even if the Sergeant's idea of holding a fort consisted of propping up the saloon bar.

"What happened, Harry? Gawd, you look tired."

"I'll have a whisky. Quarles got the papers. He told Sir H. they were proven forgeries planted on him. Whether true or not is debatable but Palabras decided not to risk it. I think the clincher was when Quarles remarked that publication would brand Palabras as a ghastly old ass."

"There is no truth on the political side. I suppose you came home with His Nibs?"

"Sir Hugh invited him for dinner."

"Love-hate as the trick cyclists say," observed the Sergeant, "but if there is anything gone bad in the kitchen I bet Quarles gets it."

"I don't propose to wait for him," said Harry. "Goodnight!"

"I'll hold the fort," said Honeybody, ogling his barmaid as if she were Gibraltar.

Harry awakened at seven, telephoned the receiving room at the Yard, dictated a report to be listened to personally by Hawker, and was down to breakfast at eight thirty. From the angle at which their table was situated, he first saw Honeybody's great face. It was clear that the Sergeant was not enjoying his usual gargantuan breakfast with relish. Then he saw, primly eating porridge and cream, Mr. Quarles, a bland look on his face. Overawed by Quarles the Sergeant had ordered prunes and rice which he was eating in small spoonfuls.

"Are you a vegetarian, Mr. James?" teased Quarles, after the good-mornings.

Harry ignored him and ordered ham and eggs.

"I have been telling the good Sergeant of its virtues."

"One does not suppose that Palabras's table groans with lettuce."

"Eight courses. He considers anything less to be low and non-eighteenth-century. I remember in 1944, when food was scarce, he used to consume six different biscuits, each of which he considered a course, after his soup and chicken. A strange fellow!"

"Hey-ho, nothing to do with me. We are away by the noon train up."

"I'm afraid not. Whitehall-wise, I rather outrank the Yard, you know, and I have *carte blanche* from dear old Hawker—he is all heart as you know—to make use of your services."

"He's an old bastard who'd sell his mother."

"Selling your mother has nothing to do with having a warm heart. But I want my final report without loose ends."

"I suppose what you told Palabras is true. Oh, yes, I told the Sergeant you got the papers back."

Honeybody engaged himself in removing a prune stone from underneath his upper denture.

"Naturally," soothed Quarles. "Of course politics *are* a trifle subjective. A Munich of today means something else tomorrow. We servants just labour on, come what may."

Honeybody felt he had to say something. "If it's a working-class practice she's a whore, Mr. James. If she's screwed by royalty or company chairmen, she's a courtesan. It's how you look at it."

"Very well put," approved Mr. Quarles. "What I want to be sure of is that Miss Sloper is tidied up and put in the file. Anything more, Sergeant?"

"The prunes were filling, sir."

"Then I'll just have some ham and eggs," said Quarles, beckoning the waitress.

Harry did not enjoy his breakfast. There was a morbid fascination in watching Mr. Quarles's pudgy little hands dissecting ham.

Quarles said suddenly: "I don't fancy your case against Beedle. I saw the local Super and he doesn't relish it, apart from the grotesquerie about the pig which would not impress a jury. No, no, listen to me," he said as Harry showed signs of interrupting, "I've had Beedle looked at in depth. He regards himself as a Thinker, and that breed does not kill—merely eggs others on. I doubt whether Lenin personally killed anything more than a few rabbits and fish."

"Who else?"

"How convenient it would be if Sir Hugh had." Quarles chuckled. "If only a case could be made against him. Miss Stinting is convinced she saw him prowling near Miss Sloper's abode."

"I would rather doubt that," said Harry. "I would not be a party to faked evidence."

"Just a joke, m'dear fellow," chuckled Quarles. "But still there is a piece missing in our jigsaw puzzle, and frankly what reputation I have rests on a capacity to deliver wholly made up jigsaw puzzles which can be bureaucratically embalmed, thus enabling our political masters, to use their cliché, to Sleep Quietly in Their Beds."

"If I may say so, Chief Inspector," said Honeybody, "it has to be somebody with access to Señor Abajo's house."

"It was often left unlocked."

"I don't fancy the idea of somebody stealing into an unlocked house, knowing where the freezer was, and spending some minutes doing the caper. That leaves Miss Drinkwater."

"You're . . ." Harry's jaw dropped.

"And who is this person?" asked Quarles sharply. He had three tones, thought Harry, smarmy, more smarmy, and whip-lash.

"She's an old Fleet-Street hand. I've known her for four or five years. She was on the *Mail*, then left for a stint on the women's mags. A good run-of-the-mill worker, so I gathered. She quit a year ago to become Palabras's factotum, arranger of speaking engagements, appointments secretary and what-have-you. About forty, married to a man I've never seen who is an engineer with the municipality."

"I think I saw her mentioned in Miss Stinting's report, a colourless dame," said Quarles.

"She hopes to be women's editor on Palabras's paper. A

pleasant person, I've always found. She is a sympathetic listener."

"Oh, dear," said Mr. Quarles, "we always suspect sympathetic listeners. We have many of 'em on our files. All those Russians we had to turf out spent their evenings drinking red wine and listening sympathetically. The human race having an endemic condition of running at the mouth, it is unnatural when you find somebody who does not."

"Nonsense," said Harry. "I think that outside work she is a little on the vague side. She could easily have admitted someone to the Abajo house—perhaps a man pretending to be a sanitary inspector or something of that kind."

"You are drawing pictures," said Quarles, shortly. "You'd better see her for a start."

"There are better suspects. General Gould, or Bruggles and his little forging friend."

"I'll tell you something, Mr. James, that you do not know."

"There are a hell of a lot of things about this case, Mr. Quarles, that I do not know."

"Listen to me. Both Gould and the actor are in the debt of Sir Hugh. Bruggles has been in debt for years—boys, champers and a diminishing amount of work add up to that. Sir Hugh takes up his paper. Oh, I suppose Bruggles owes him twenty thousand pounds. As for Gould, he nearly came a cropper once, a nasty business. Palabras was enjoying one of his short war-time spells in the Government sun, and for some reason he saved the purblind fool. Since then Gould has been his creature, whether he likes it or not."

"After all these years?"

"Gould was the youngest man ever to hold his rank, apart from the first Churchill. No man in his old age likes to be exposed as a cowardly, half-treacherous time-server. It boils down to the fact that Palabras is far too cautious to employ these two characters to shoot anybody. Their obligations to him would immediately place Hugh under suspicion. He would either do it himself or employ a professional."

"There aren't any pro gunmen in the country that I know of," said Harry. "There are four who work out of Amsterdam, but the Customs have damn great photos of them hanging up. As for Americans, they'd stick out like a sore thumb."

"I'd like you to see Miss Drinkwater."

"Oh, I'll see her," said Harry, conscious that he was sulky. "I think she mentioned that she starts work at ten, old Palabras liking to go through his mail and the papers first. Meantime I'd like a peaceful breakfast."

Quarles demolished the last of his toast and beckoned the waiter. "I'll leave you in digestive peace and make some phone calls."

"Harry," said Honeybody, after he had gone. "Proper old bastard, ain't he? He frightened me into ordering those goddamned prunes. Do you think I could risk a couple of kippers?"

"Go your disgusting way," said Harry, confining himself to toast and marmalade. There was something about Quarles.

The butler was less pleased than ever when he saw Harry and Honeybody on Sir Hugh Palabras's porch. "Miss Drinkwater is not in."

"Could we wait?"

"Outside," said the butler. "I don't suppose I can prevent you lurkin' outside as long as you don't spit or cause a nuisance."

"What's this?" said Sir Hugh, coming up behind him. "Police again! I am pretty well fed up with these constant visitations."

"This is the last, sir, and we would like a word with Miss Drinkwater."

"She's late, which is unusual. Oh, well, you'd better come in and have coffee."

Sir Hugh's living-room was broad and so designed as to trap the sun.

"What do you want to see her about?"

"This blasted pig and the rifle barrel within."

"She told me that she had made quite a few pounds out of filing the story." Sir Hugh chuckled. "She showed a lightish touch I did not know she had. Her stuff is generally heavyish, which suits me, as the speeches as I write them occasionally slip into the frivolous."

"I knew her around Fleet Street, an assiduous reporter. I wondered how you came to employ her."

"She evidently gets around. A year ago when I got this idea of buying a paper, she came to me, suggesting she could take care of women's features, on a more serious plane than the usual hot-pants and *paella* formula. It takes time to buy a paper: she apparently thought it was like going to Woolworth's. But I'd had a falling-out with the P.R. firm I dealt with, so I thought I might as well engage Drinkwater full time. One of the best things I ever did. An agency in Granchester send a short-hand writer over three days a week, but Drinkwater doesn't mind doing the urgent stuff. I get a lot of letters, of course, some most confidential, and it's a treat to have somebody thoroughly trustworthy to process them. I was in trouble once when a girl had one too many in a pub and started talking about my business. Drinkwater is a misnomer: you couldn't get her tight." Sir Hugh poured out the coffee.

"How's that wretch Beedle?" he asked. "Why the deuce you gave him bail I'll never fathom. I went over yesterday evening and the blighter opened the door. Abajo thinks it's funny—there is a Spanish saying, apparently, about a fine stew covering a multitude of sins. Not that he isn't a fine cook, or would be but for Abajo's queer tastes. Sheep's head *de Burgos* they served me once. Delicious, but the eyes kept leering at you. More coffee? And where is that woman?"

"As far as Beedle is concerned," said Harry with a hateful look at Honeybody, shamelessly ogling a tantalus upon a sideboard, "there is no place where a black man without a passport can run. But I would be grateful if you would ring Miss Drinkwater's home."

A telephone extension was in the corner of the room. Sir Hugh dialled twice. "No answer," he said and looked worried.

"She has a husband. I've never met him, a reticulation engineer, I think."

"As far as I remember she never talked about him. He must work in the Granchester Town Hall, but what the devil is his name? Never mind."

Masterfully, Sir Hugh got the Town Clerk. "A fellow of sewage and water. Married to a woman who works for me. What say? Speak up, man. You can't have many crapper cleaners! I suppose he came from London a year ago." Palabras fumed for a couple of minutes, then, "You're Miss Drinkwater's husband? This is Hugh Palabras. I'm worried because your wife didn't turn up for work today. London? Me? Not so. Thanks very much." He slammed down the receiver.

"Bloody fellow is named Strapdriver, sounds like a gnat peeing on a tin. His wife left for London last night, by the nine o'clock from Granchester, saying she was going for two days on my business."

"When did she leave here yesterday?"

"I don't know. She had a free hand. I have implicit confidence in her. Nevertheless it's strange."

"I suppose there is nothing missing?"

"Nonsense! She has had ample opportunity to steal a small fortune. I may seem casual and in fact I don't like possessions endlessly hanging round my neck, but I have a pretty good idea exactly what I own down to the last thousand. I suppose it's a man: she's at the age when they go silly."

"Did she know about the file?"

Sir Hugh showed some unease. "I have an editor picked out, but I was in the habit of discussing journalism generally with her. I told her we'd start with a few stories which would set the cat among the Establishment and now that you have mentioned it, she seemed rather knowing, though I supposed it to be expertise. She knows everybody, it seems."

"I'd better see the husband," said Harry, "and I'd better have her address. She just might return home."

The house belonging to Miss Drinkwater and her husband was a post-war mistake. On one level it had a pre-fabricated look, like a cosmetic plastic face-lift which had not worn very well. It was one of a complex of twenty called 'The Close'. The front gardens were spacious but generally indicative of busy people with little time to spare. Honeybody reported that there was nothing on the clothes line: Harry's hammering at the door yielded nothing.

"Anything wrong?" asked a querulous voice. It was the next-door neighbour, elderly, male, and probably interested in stamps.

"Do you know Miss Drinkwater, as she is called by her maiden name?"

"Police?"

"Well, yes."

"I'm a retired debt-collector. You get to know all sorts." The mottled face peered at them over the fence. "Second sight, so they say. I can tell whether a man'll pay or try to dodge. I wouldn't trust her if I did have a signature with witnesses."

"Does she have many visitors?"

"Quite a lot—long-haired. Me and the wife don't approve. When I was collecting I used to take them by the short hairs, as the Good Book counsels." He gave a chuckle and shuffled away.

"Neighbours are always like that," said Honeybody, "Gawd knows why."

"There are not any nice people in the world," said Harry. "We'll proceed to interview the happy husband."

"No such animal after the first week," grunted Honeybody, whose rawboned helpmate was indeed formidable.

An aura of terror surrounded Granchester Town Hall, emanating from the Town Clerk, a fearsome man with red side-whiskers. Having reduced Harry to a state of saying "yes, sir," he relented, expatiated on the possible misuse of public time, and arranged for them to see Mr. Strapdriver in the interview room, which smelled of lye and the deadened hopes of generations of ratepayers.

Strapdriver was large and nervous. Harry thought there might be a faint smell of gin. About fifty, greying, amiable and vague.

"Your wife, sir, might be able to fill us in a bit about the killing of Miss Sloper."

"She's in London, about business for old Palabras."

"Sir Hugh told me that is not the case."

"Then probably I got it wrong. Clever woman, she does a certain amount of free-lance—helps towards the annual holiday." Strapdriver had the contented look of men with working wives.

"I've forgotten when you got married?" lied Harry who had never known.

"Four years. Never regretted it—a magnificent cook, but, then, of course she's not English." Strapdriver chuckled amiably.

Harry felt a twinge of the cold sweats, but kept his nerve. "I never dreamed that she was anything but English."

"A refugee in 1938. Polish."

"Where does she stay in London?"

"She has one surviving relative, an aunt. I'll scribble you the address." Strapdriver produced a folded scratchpad from an inner pocket.

"You wouldn't have thought she was foreign, Harry," said Honeybody as they walked out.

"Ten per cent of the population, more or less, are, and most have no accent. Drinkwater, a translation of a very common Polish name! I don't like it at all."

Neither did Mr. Quarles when they saw him. "A proper dog's dinner," he said, scratching at his second little chin in a disapproving way. "Get a line to Hawker and keep it open," he said. "I'll O.K. the cost."

Hawker was in his groaning mood. "I remember her, about forty-seven, neutral hair, blue eyes, not much chin, thin, but with good legs. Pleasant—she interviewed me once. Have you a photo?"

Harry cursed himself and from his own room got through to Granchester Town Hall. "Mai wife has a kind of allergy to being photographed," bleated Mr. Strapdriver.

"That's all we want," said Hawker. "A bod that does not wish to be photographed is like an accountant who never takes a holiday. All right. Ask Quarles to alert his infernal staff."

It was a matter of sitting and waiting as the clock crept round. At noon an impersonal voice reeled off some facts: "The address given by Strapdriver did not exist. Miss Drinkwater's colleagues have noticed her repugnance to photography—most of them dote on having their photograph at the head of an article. We did pick up a rather poor one taken at the opening of an hotel. She seems to have tried to shuffle out of camera range, but we had it blown up and circulated. This includes Quarles's people."

At two the call was for Quarles. He hesitated and repeated it word for word: "Drinkwater rather resembles a Chinese agent spotted in Hong Kong in 1956. There was a Drinkwater, a refugee orphan in London in the 'forties, but little is known about her. The records were destroyed by enemy action. The evidence appears to be that she dropped out of sight around 1955. The Drinkwater you refer to in fact worked on a Hong Kong paper, spoke perfect English, had a pleasant personality, and was one of many Caucasians in the pay of China. In the scale of ten points, she ranked eight. In June, 1960, she dropped out of sight. Apparently she turned up in London in the December and freelanced until she got a job on a paper. She did not mention any Asiatic experience."

"Where does that leave us?" demanded Quarles as he put down the handset.

"The airports," said Harry, wearily. "She'll run for it, the dear, helpful darling! I could kick myself."

"These shrewd bitches can always fool you," stated Honeybody. "I remember a motherly old landlady I once had who turned out to have fifteen convictions for procuring. I was a lonely lad in London, and it fair burned me that the service was turned on, as it were, but I never knew until the Ser'nt came round and took her in for possessing cocaine."

"No point in staying here," said Quarles. "We'll wait until Hawker comes through."

At three the old Superintendent came through directly. "This fellow, Strapdriver, is genuine. He hails from near Granchester, was in the Army from 1944 to early 'forty-six, got an engineering degree at the Polytechnic, and had jobs in

Aberdeen, Edinburgh and London, where he met Miss Drinkwater. He married first in 1949, but divorced his wife in 1951—she ran away with a bookmaker. Generally a model of efficiency in his work, not very capable in his private life, a bumbling sort of case, and a mildly enthusiastic Tory—drives old people to the booths when cometh the great day. He has never been involved in classified work, is not in debt except for five hundred pounds still owing on his bungalow. Moderate potus, though likes a glass of gin, not a woman-chaser, no boys, does not bet. I suppose Drinkwater married him for a cover. Her 'best friend' in Fleet Street is a proper old bitch who says that Strapdriver was happy to do exactly what he was told. She ran the social side of their life. Strapdriver often worked during the evenings. That's all."

Harry repeated it. Quarles pursed his mouth. "We'd better be getting along."

Harry rather doubted they would ever see Miss Drinkwater again, but something went wrong, notably an accident to the Dublin ferry, the most convenient and quick method of getting to safety. Instead the spotter in an upstairs window at London Airport, with his five-foot telescope, turned to his mate at eight o'clock next morning and said: "Red-headed, middle-aged woman on the Milan flight. She looks like her"—he jerked his thumb to one of the clip-boards with the blown-up, tinted photographs.

Miss Drinkwater was inclined to argue with the suave officials who ushered her off the plane in a smokescreen of double-talk. She had come, not perhaps to the end of the road, but to the end of one of the devious lanes of her life.

She had taken off her red wig by the time Harry and Quarles arrived.

"Twirling my moustache, Joan, I say 'so we meet again'!" said Harry.

"Briefly one hopes." Miss Drinkwater had dispensed with her old soft personality.

"This is Mr. Quarles!"

She gave the pudgy man the faintest of knowing nods.

"Mrs. Strapdriver, or Miss Drinkwater, whichever you wish to use, I shall have to detain you touching the matter of the death of one Miss Phoebe Sloper."

"I thought you had Beedle in for that. You can hardly detain the whole of the West Country."

"He has been let out. Have you an alibi for the time when Miss Sloper was killed?"

"No, my husband frequently has to work until midnight. But what is your evidence?"

"Flight in a red wig and a passport made out to a Mrs. Geralton, who lost it in Paris last autumn, are a couple of the premisses."

"I am on confidential business for Sir Hugh Palabras."

"He denies it," said Harry. "Miss Sloper, who you knew well, had the quixotic idea of getting the missing file back—oh, you know all about it—so you shot her, a typical pro job."

"You'll look a fool in court."

"There is no need for us to get hot under our collars—bras, one supposes, in the case of ladies." Mr. Quarles gave his chuckle. "We do wish to handle this in a co-operative way."

"Such as what co-operation?" Miss Drinkwater sounded tired and for the first time she flinched from Quarles's bland little glances.

"We have two people in a gaol outside Peking. Two for one, but you are more important, being graded as eight, whereas our own operatives raise seven between them. On the other hand of course, it might not be pleasant for you—failure not being a highly regarded commodity. We might be able to arrange an alternative."

"I'd take Peking," she said. "At least the food is better."

"A little stay in a place we have in Scotland," said Mr. Quarles, "quite voluntary on your part. It's a nursing home, so you can have a nice rest. One imagines the exchange will be made in Albania. Is your husband the kind of man to squeak?"

"He likes a quiet life and the occasional meal, and as long as the gin bottle is on the sideboard he does not complain. If you had a motherly woman to look after him he would not notice I'd gone. Palabras cannot talk."

Quarles got up and bowed as the three brawny police matrons who had come with him entered.

Miss Drinkwater broke down and cried unpleasantly.

"I never like to hear women snivel," said Quarles, as he shut the door. "But of course she won't have much of a future in Peking, though we'll put in a good word for her. I dare say a couple of sherries in the V.I.P. bar won't do us any harm."

Quarles did it properly and ordered a bottle of *La Ina*.

"But what about Miss Sloper?" asked Harry.

"Boy!" said Quarles, "public memory lasts ten days—that's the whole nub of our existence." He nibbled a piece of smoked salmon. "However, you might say old Sloper finally earned her keep quite handsomely."